JAGGED INK - SPECIAL EDITION

A MONTGOMERY INK: COLORADO SPRINGS NOVEL

CARRIE ANN RYAN

Jagged Ink
A Montgomery Ink: Colorado Springs Novel
By: Carrie Ann Ryan
© 2019 Carrie Ann Ryan

This book is a work of fiction. Names, characters, places, and incidents either are products of the author's imagination or are used fictitiously. Any resemblance to actual events, locales or persons, living or dead, is entirely coincidental.
No part of this book can be reproduced in any form or by electronic or mechanical means including information storage and retrieval systems, without the express written permission of the author. The only exception is by a reviewer who may quote short excerpts in a review.

All content warnings are listed on the book page for this book on my website.

NO AI TRAINING: Without in any way limiting the author's [and publisher's] exclusive rights under copyright, any use of this publication to "train" generative artificial intelligence (AI) technologies to generate text is expressly prohibited. The author reserves all rights to license uses of this work for generative AI training and development of machine learning language models.

PRAISE FOR CARRIE ANN RYAN....

"Carrie Ann Ryan knows how to pull your heartstrings and make your pulse pound! Her wonderful Redwood Pack series will draw you in and keep you reading long into the night. I can't wait to see what comes next with the new generation, the Talons. Keep them coming, Carrie Ann!" –Lara Adrian, New York Times bestselling author of CRAVE THE NIGHT

"Carrie Ann Ryan never fails to draw readers in with passion, raw sensuality, and characters that pop off the page. Any book by Carrie Ann is an absolute treat." – New York Times Bestselling Author J. Kenner

"With snarky humor, sizzling love scenes, and brilliant, imaginative worldbuilding, The Dante's Circle series reads as if Carrie Ann Ryan peeked at my personal wish list!" – NYT Bestselling Author, Larissa Ione

"Carrie Ann Ryan writes sexy shifters in a world full of passionate happily-ever-afters." – *New York Times* Bestselling Author Vivian Arend

"Carrie Ann's books are sexy with characters you can't help but love from page one. They are heat and heart blended to perfection." *New York Times* Bestselling Author Jayne Rylon

Carrie Ann Ryan's books are wickedly funny and deliciously hot, with plenty of twists to keep you guessing. They'll keep you up all night!" USA Today Bestselling Author Cari Quinn

"Once again, Carrie Ann Ryan knocks the Dante's Circle series out of the park. The queen of hot, sexy, enthralling paranormal romance, Carrie Ann is an author not to miss!" *New York Times* bestselling Author Marie Harte

DEDICATION

To Dan.
I miss you so much.
Thank you for teaching me what it means to be married,
and the work it takes to make sure we were who we needed
to be.

JAGGED INK

The Montgomery Ink: Colorado Springs series continues with a couple fighting to keep what they thought they had and gain what they didn't know they needed.

Roxie Montgomery met her soul mate when she least expected it. When he asked her to marry him, she thought her happily ever after was only just beginning. Then, she found that walking into the sunset was much harder than her favorite books made it out to be. After a crushing loss, she feels as though she doesn't know her husband anymore, or rather...she doesn't know herself.

Carter Marshall has loved Roxie since the first time he saw her. But as the days pass between them, so does the distance. He doesn't know how to show her that he's all in, and honestly doesn't know if she's in at all. When an accident changes everything, they'll have to decide if what they have can be salvaged, or if starting over is the answer. Or even possible.

Without fighting, without a true new beginning, sometimes, the remnants of what was lost can leave anyone jagged, shells of what they were before. It will take more than the idea of forever for Roxie and Carter to find themselves again, but as the Montgomerys know, nothing worth fighting for is easy.

CHAPTER ONE

Fire burned, bright and hot.

Those were the first things that had come to Carter Marshall's mind when the explosion hit.

He hadn't thought of what might happen, not even for a moment, when he threw himself on top of Thea's body, trying to take the brunt of the heat.

But the *heat*.

It was so fucking hot.

Carter snorted to himself, thinking about that. Of course, fire was hot. Of course, it burned. Of course, it singed. Thankfully, he hadn't been able to scent his own skin burning. But he had been able to smell burnt flour and other baked goods as the industrial bakery oven exploded in front of them.

He'd heard screams, mostly coming from Thea, and maybe from himself. He'd heard people rushing towards them. He'd heard other people crying out.

He had heard it all, but he hadn't really felt much.

Maybe he wasn't supposed to feel anything. Maybe, in that moment, it had been how it was supposed to be.

At least that's what he'd thought when he attempted not to feel, when he tried to make sure Thea was okay and ensure he could *maybe* walk out of the inferno.

And then he'd woken up, and he hadn't been dead.

And he hadn't been alone.

Roxie had been there.

The Montgomerys had been there.

He hadn't been alone.

And for someone who'd thought he always would be, that was a comfort. At least...it had been.

Someone had tried to destroy part of his sister-in-law's bakery, Colorado Icing. And in doing so, that person had almost killed the love of his life's sister. Had nearly killed Thea. And had almost killed him.

Now, he sat in a hospital bed, wondering what the fuck to do, because the explosion was only the beginning.

The heat, the flames, yes, they burned brightly and quickly.

But the dull ache running down his side and in his heart...that was what would last. *That* he would have to deal with.

"Are you okay over there?" Mace asked, his brows drawn. Carter turned to look at the other man with his dark hair and inked skin peeking out from under his shirt sleeves. Mace had been there for over an hour, just waiting. Waiting like all of them were doing.

Carter almost shrugged to say that he was okay, then stopped himself just in time. He had pretty severe burns down his side and leg, even some on his neck. And, because of that, shrugging would likely hurt like hell.

He would be okay. The doctors had told him that over and over again. He didn't even have to worry about infection as much as he might have if he had been in the fire even a second longer. But because the flames had gone overhead, and he had flattened himself as much as possible over Thea's body, he was going to be okay. Well, as okay as he could be with severe burns down his side, though, thankfully not life-threatening ones. And he had full mobility, or he would. *I will be okay*, he repeated to himself.

Theoretically.

Finally, he answered Mace. "I'm fine. Just tired." He didn't ask the question he wanted to. Didn't ask the question that he should have the minute he woke up and saw Mace by his side.

It was the second day after the explosion, and when he was asleep through his surgery, things had gone to hell and back with his family. Thea had discharged herself from the hospital, thankfully, not as hurt as he was. Then, she'd gone off to see what had happened to her boyfriend as he had left her side and hadn't come back. Apparently, Dimitri had gotten hurt in another accident and was even now in the same hospital as Carter.

The Montgomerys sure liked coming to medical centers.

Carter should know that, he had married a Montgomery after all, and he had spent more time in hospitals with Roxie than he cared to admit. He swallowed down bile from the pain, tried to push the thoughts from his head. He had to do that often when it came to Roxie. Not think. Not dwell.

It was better for both of them. He just focused on the now, and not the past...and sure as hell not the future.

Mace leaned forward in his chair, his expression concerned. "You want me to get you something?"

Carter shook his head, at least as much as he was able. "I'm fine. Just bored." True. Somewhat.

Mace snorted. "Well, I'm not going to lie, I'm glad you're bored. Because you're here and able to be bored."

"I guess that's true. If I have time to be bored, I guess I have time to heal. I'd just rather be home while I do it."

But as soon as Carter said the words, he wasn't sure that was true. Home was awkward, it wasn't easy. Home was full of memories, the depth of them piled on top of one another like coats of paint that had never been chipped away.

Taking away his breath.

He was suffocating, trying to figure out what to say, trying not to step on toes—even his own. He hated it, but he didn't know how to stop it. Didn't know how to make things better.

He didn't know if there *was* a better.

It would be easier if he didn't love Roxie. Things were always easier if love wasn't in the equation.

"Carter?"

He pulled himself from his thoughts again. He needed to. "What?"

Mace's voice was low and far too careful. "Her mom sent her home. Said she needed to take a shower and get some sleep. She's been in the waiting room or by your side since she ran into the ER after we all found out about the accident. You know she'd be here if she could. But the folks pretty much dragged her out of the room to get herself together, and that's why I'm here."

Carter couldn't think about that right then. He didn't want her to see him like this. He already felt like only part of a man most days he saw her. This way? Weak, and not himself? He didn't want to do that to her.

"Where's Daisy?"

The *she* they had been talking about was Roxie, of course, but they could come back to that. The fact that Carter's brother-in-law—or his soon-to-be brother-in-law if Mace and Adrienne had anything to say about it—was there, was nice. But the man had a daughter at home. He was the sole provider for the child ever since Daisy's mom ran out on her. Between Adrienne and Mace, and the rest of the Montgomerys, there was always child care, but Carter didn't like pulling Mace away from his kid.

"She's with my sisters. They drove down from Denver," Mace replied. Carter nodded, thankful that Mace's two sisters had come to help out. He knew they didn't see their niece very much and were trying to make the hour and a half trip more often, but still, he didn't really like the fact that everyone had to change their plans because of him.

He decided to change the subject. "So, they caught the person that did it? The sabotage."

Mace nodded. "Yeah, there was the one person who actually did it, but the person that orchestrated it... Molly? She is going to either be behind bars or getting the help she needs. She attacked Dimitri, too, in their old home. So something was definitely off there. But it makes me so fucking angry that it even got to this point. She could have hurt a lot more people. She *did* hurt a lot of people."

"I'm just glad Thea wasn't alone back there, you know?" Carter said, picking at some of the fuzz on his hospital blanket.

"I don't think any of us want to think about it. Adrienne's ready to bust some kneecaps I think, she's so damn angry."

"Well, your girl stood up for herself when she needed to, and she wants to stand up for others whenever she can. She could pretty much kick my ass if she wanted to."

"I think she could kick all our asses, especially with you down for the count right now. But you're going to be okay, you're going to be right back to fighting shape and ready to kick all of our asses soon. Especially considering that out of the four of us—Dimitri, me, Shep and you—you're pretty much the most built."

"Well, with my job, I have to be."

"That's the truth, with two tattoo artists and a teacher, the mechanic who has to lift things other than a pencil or pen all day is probably going to be the one with the most muscle."

"It's going to be okay, Carter, make sure you tell your wife that," Mace said, his voice low.

Carter didn't say anything then, knowing that Mace was fishing. They all were. Everyone wanted to know what was going on between Roxie and Carter. And he hated the fact that he didn't have answers for them. He saw the looks, heard the whispers. He wasn't the dumb mechanic that others often thought of him as.

The Montgomerys may love him, may have taken him into their family when he didn't have anyone else, but he still wasn't one of them. Not really. He was the guy who had gone to mechanic school and took a couple of business classes to open up his shop. He was the guy that had fallen in love with someone he never thought would actually love him back.

And he was the guy who had gotten married because he thought he was making the right decision, who had thought he was doing it because everything would be better for it. Because he loved her.

And people wondered about the reasons behind it.

It wasn't any of their goddamn business.

Carter loved Roxie Montgomery.

He just didn't know if love was enough anymore.

"I'm going to go get a soda or something. Shep will be in soon to take over. You want anything?"

"I'm fine. I can call the nurses if I need anything, but I think I'm just going to take a nap or something."

Carter didn't want to talk to anyone, didn't really want anyone near him. All he wanted to do was heal and figure out what the fucking next step was. Something he had been thinking about forever it seemed. What was the next step with his business? What was the next step with his life? What was the next step with the woman who wouldn't talk to him?

"Roxie should be here soon too, you know," Mace said as he stepped toward the door. "I don't think her mom is going to keep her away for too long. I'm pretty sure they had to drag her out, and probably scared the nurses and staff in order for her to actually leave. But she'll be back."

"Yeah, she will." Carter didn't say anything else as Mace left, he could only wonder how long Roxie would stay when she came back.

He hated this. Hated not knowing anything. That was always the problem, the not knowing, the feeling of being two steps behind like he was a fucking idiot. But more and more these days, every time he thought about his wife, he couldn't help but feel stupid. And that was on his shoulders, that was never on her. But he would have to figure out what to do about this feeling.

But, deep down in his gut, he knew that the accident would only make things harder for everybody.

Carter settled in for a nap and noticed that Shep, Roxie's brother, walked in, checked on him, and then left again. A couple of other people came in, and he figured they were nurses and doctors. He was just so damned tired. His body exhausted, hurting. His mind hurting. His heart hurting.

He hated feeling like this. He was a man who worked with his hands, someone who knew what the fuck he was doing when it came to what was in front of him. But what surrounded him, what was behind him and lurking? That, he couldn't stop thinking about. That was what he couldn't control. And he was afraid everything he couldn't control would end up slipping through his fingers.

A few hours later, the door opened, and Carter knew *she* was there before he saw her. Even over the scent of antiseptic and all the ointments on his body, he knew it was her. She tried different perfumes and lotions, but there was always just the smell of Roxie. The one that was uniquely her, sweet and a little floral. Maybe a little spice on certain days. It didn't matter what she was wearing, how long her day had been, or how long she went without a shower. It was just Roxie.

His Roxie.

Carter resisted rubbing his hand over his heart at the thought. His Roxie wasn't really a phrase he could use anymore, was it?

She hadn't been his for a while, no matter what the paperwork said.

Damn, he hated himself.

And he couldn't help but wonder...if he hated himself for any longer, would he end up hating her, too?

"You're awake," Roxie said, her voice soft, hesitant.

She was always so cautious around him.

Where had the woman gone who was such a force? Where did the woman who couldn't keep her hands off him—just like he couldn't do with her—go?

"I am."

He didn't know what to say after that. How could he not know what to say to the woman he loved with everything he had? What the hell was wrong with them?

Or rather, what the hell was wrong with him?

He just needed to open his mouth and say something. Anything. Tell her how he felt. That he loved her. That he wanted to work this out. That they could figure out whatever *this* was. But he didn't know how to do that. Not when she looked so unhappy, so...not Roxie around him.

He didn't want to force her to love him. Didn't want to push her to be with him. To speak to him. To tell him her fears when he knew deep down that *he* was her fear.

He was going to lose everything he'd ever wanted, and he wasn't sure how to deal with that. It wasn't like he was dealing with it well at the moment.

Carter looked into her deep blue eyes and willed himself not to beg. It wouldn't do either of them any good, and with the pain meds he was on, he was afraid he'd say something senseless.

When she came to sit down next to him, he just turned his head and stared at her, wanting to keep her on his mind and in his memories, feeling like the time was too short for them. Seconds and moments were passing in a blink, like sand between the fingers as it fell, and he couldn't hold on any longer.

She reached out and put her hand on his, and he almost moved his away, startled at not only her movement but also his reaction. He turned his hand over and clasped hers as if knowing it might be forever if he let go.

"The doctors said you would be okay. That you can

come home soon." She wasn't looking at his face but their joined hands.

He didn't want to let go.

He never wanted to let go.

He cleared his throat and looked at her face, willing her to look at him. "That's what I hear. Maybe another night or two while they get me ready for PT and are sure that I don't catch an infection, and then I can come home."

She gave him a tight nod, still not looking directly at him. "I'm...I'm glad." She cleared her throat again. "I...I'm so sorry you got hurt, Carter. I can't believe it all happened like it did. I don't know what I would have done if—" She didn't finish her statement, but she didn't need to.

He didn't know what he'd do if he lost her either.

Just thinking those words made him want to throw up.

"I'm okay, Roxie."

She looked up at the sound of her name, and he realized he hadn't said it aloud in far too long. He needed to change that. Needed to change a lot of things.

But, sometimes, there was no going back.

"I don't like seeing you hurt."

"I don't like being hurt."

"Thank you." She licked her lips. "Thank you for saving my sister." She wiped away a tear, and it wasn't lost on him that he hadn't seen her cry for him, but for her sister. Maybe it was all too much for her, or perhaps it was because she didn't love him enough to break through that barrier of hers.

"Thea's family," he said, watching Roxie's face for her reaction.

She just nodded, still looking partly down at their clasped hands. "And you're the kind of guy who will throw yourself in harm's way for family, for strangers, for...everyone." She let out a shaky breath. "You're a good man, Carter."

He didn't know why those words hurt. They shouldn't. But then again, most things hurt these days.

They sat in silence for a few more moments and then talked about the family, never themselves. They were good at that. Talking without saying anything. He didn't know how to fix things without hurting her.

He'd just hurt himself instead.

It took five more days for him to go home, and he knew PT and recovery wouldn't be easy. It was going to take time. Time he didn't have with his shop, though his crew was working hard for him. Time he didn't have because he knew it would be hard on his wife.

But he'd push through.

It wasn't like he had a choice.

Roxie drove them home, having told the rest of her family she could handle it. He didn't mind since he didn't want to deal with the others watching them, trying to see what was going on beneath the surface. He just wanted to be alone, wanted to heal. And he wanted to fix what was going on between him and his wife.

When they walked inside, he winced every few steps, going slow as he tried to catch his breath.

"Here, let me help," Roxie said after she'd closed the front door. She slid under his good arm and pressed against his unmarred side, taking some of his weight. "Lean on me, I've got you."

Oh, how he wished that were true.

Because he wasn't looking at her now.

Wasn't even truly feeling her.

Instead, he looked at the hutch to the side of the entryway, to the stack of papers and folders that hadn't been there before he was hurt. To the mail that had been delivered in pristine and professional envelopes.

He knew that company.

Knew the name on the label.

And he knew exactly what it was.

He couldn't look at his wife. At his Roxie.

Because he'd been right.

She wasn't his.

Because those papers meant it was over.

"Were you going to tell me about the divorce papers, or were you just going to wait and see if I saw them?" he asked, his voice devoid of emotion.

When she didn't say anything, he moved away from her, walked away.

He couldn't fix this.

No one could.

He'd lost his Montgomery, his heart.

And there was no going back.

CHAPTER TWO

Roxie Montgomery couldn't breathe. How could she have been so careless? So damn stupid. In her rush to get to the hospital to pick Carter up after work, and dealing with issue after issue, she'd forgotten that she'd tossed the mail on the table without even looking at it.

How could she have missed the heavy weight of the decision on her heart and in her hands as she rushed to Carter's side?

Roxie looked to where Carter slowly limped away and forced herself not to run after him. Forced herself not to give him an explanation. Because it wasn't like she had one to give.

Her head hurt, her body ached, and she hadn't slept well in what felt like years. But she truly hadn't slept well since hearing that Carter had been hurt. It didn't matter that her mother had tried to tuck her in like she was a little girl and tried to make her go to sleep so she would have enough energy to deal with what was to come. But there wasn't enough fortitude in the world to deal with what was to come. After all, she barely had enough to deal with what was happening now.

She couldn't believe that she'd left the paperwork out, couldn't grasp that she hadn't even noticed it. She'd had to head into the office because she needed to send out a few year-end things that she couldn't get out of. They were a small group, and she had to work longer hours than most to make sure she could rise up in the company ranks—and even just to prove to herself that she was good at what she did.

And though she could have handed the paperwork off to someone else, she either couldn't let anyone else handle it, couldn't do that to her clients, or she was afraid of what would happen as soon as she walked into Carter's room.

Because it was always so awkward with him lately, even if she didn't mean for that to be the case.

She hated awkward. Hated what had become of them. And now it was only going to get worse.

But after she did what she needed to do, she had run from her office, the place she had gone to for a single client, a single piece of paper, and had gone to Carter's side again so she could help him come home. He hadn't wanted her by his side anyway, hadn't wanted her near him when he was trying to heal.

She didn't know if it was because he didn't want her to see him weak, because Carter was anything but weak, or if it was because he just didn't want her there at all.

Because she knew the way things had been for the past few months, she was afraid it was the latter.

She was always afraid it was the latter.

So, after she had come home for just a few minutes following the office before going to get Carter, she had checked the mail but just tossed it on the entryway table. She hadn't even noticed that the bundle was heavier than usual—the envelope she had been waiting for far heavier in weight of memory and meaning than the paper itself.

She hadn't noticed any of it because she had been too worried about Carter and what she was going to say if he really was able to come home.

All she could do was picture him lying on the bed, sleeping, his face relaxed. Because he never looked relaxed these days. Between work and everything going on between them, there was always that little furrow between his brows as if he were thinking about something that made him hurt. Thinking so hard that he didn't know what to say to her. But it wasn't like she knew what to say to him either.

They weren't the same people they were when they got married. Weren't the same people they had been when they went on their first date.

And, apparently, they weren't even the same people as before the accident.

Roxie's hands shook. She quickly reached up to wipe away a tear, annoyed with herself for even letting the pain show. She couldn't cry over him, couldn't let herself feel anything more than she already did or she would break. Because she missed him so much—everything about him, even just the idea of him. And she'd almost lost him.

Not only had her sister nearly died, but Roxie had almost lost her husband, as well.

The husband she didn't know anymore.

The husband that she was afraid she would have to say goodbye to because there wasn't much left to hold onto.

People said it was easy just to talk out your problems, that everything could be fixed with just a simple conversation. Well, that wasn't the case. Because the hard part was determining what the other person would say once you talked to them. And Roxie didn't want to know.

No, that wasn't right.

She *already* knew.

And she was afraid that once she heard those words, she wouldn't be *Roxie* anymore.

And that was selfish.

She needed to grow a pair and *not* be selfish.

But...but it wasn't that easy.

She didn't want to hear the words that he didn't love her anymore. Didn't want to hear the words that he didn't know the person she'd become. She didn't want to hear the words that the reason they had gotten married wasn't there anymore and there was no use pretending that everything they had wasn't balancing on a precipice, looking out over an abyss, praying there was light in the darkness.

When people told you that you just needed to talk out your problems and that everything would be smoothed over, they weren't the ones who actually had to speak. They weren't the ones who had to form the words. They weren't the ones that had to figure out what to say to discover how they were feeling or sit there and listen when someone told you they didn't love you anymore.

Or, maybe, that love wasn't enough.

Because Roxie thought Carter might still love her, though maybe not the same *her* that she was now.

Because after everything that had happened, she couldn't be the same.

She couldn't be the Roxie that had started the relationship. She couldn't be the woman that had first formed the attraction.

And she didn't know if she wanted to be that person anymore.

But she also knew that she didn't like who she was now. If she didn't like herself, how was Carter supposed to?

So, she pushed those thoughts out of her head and traced her finger along the envelope that told her that her marriage was over. Because Carter had seen it. There was no going back.

She had to let him go because she loved him with every ounce of her being. Because, sometimes, fighting just ended up being even harder.

Because, sometimes, fighting meant breaking yourself in two, and Roxie didn't have much of herself left to give.

She hadn't meant for him to see the paperwork this way, although she hadn't been able to figure out how to show it to him at all. Things just weren't working for them, and it was better to cut their losses before they ended up hating each other or hurting each other even more than they already had. It would be easier for both of them if they just walked away. Because they hadn't gotten married for the right reasons, and she sure as hell didn't want to stay married for the worst of them.

But before she could do any of that, she needed to make sure Carter was okay. Because he had almost died to save her sister, and she'd be damned if she forced him out of the house, or forced him to stay in this house alone while he was still healing. He deserved far more than that because he was still the man she married—at least parts of him were.

She could figure out the rest later.

After all, that's what she had been telling herself every day for over a year.

She rolled her shoulders back, ran her hands down her blouse, trying to straighten out the wrinkles that weren't there, and made her way back to where Carter had gone.

The master bedroom was on the second floor, and she wasn't sure that he had the energy or the strength to make it up there.

So, he'd gone to the guest room. She didn't know why that hurt so much.

It wasn't as if they had touched when they had slept together in the same bed recently. They had been two strangers sleeping side by side, trying not to talk about what was important while ignoring everything that was.

Roxie hated that she couldn't tell Carter what she thought, because the problem was, she didn't know. Maybe if she had some space, she could figure it out. But there wasn't time for that. She wasn't going to force him to be with her when, in the end, they'd break each other. They needed the space they so desperately tried to avoid.

She swallowed back a sob, just like she had before when it came to him. She couldn't cry. Not now. Not ever. Her feelings didn't matter here. Just making sure that he was healthy and alive. Once that happened, they could figure out the next step.

It didn't matter that she hated herself with each passing day.

It didn't matter that she felt that he was going to hate her.

Because that's just who they were. They were Roxie and Carter, the enigma of the Colorado Springs Montgomerys.

And she wasn't sure they actually loved each other anymore.

She loved the *idea* of him, but she didn't really know

him anymore. So how could she fall in love with someone that she didn't know?

How could she stay in love with a man that she didn't recognize?

"Carter?"

"Back here," he said from the guest bathroom. She nodded, even though he couldn't see her, and made her way back to him, toeing off her shoes as she did.

"Can I help you with anything?"

"Not sure what I need you to help with." His voice was rough.

"Carter," she whispered the word, not sure what else to say.

"Not really sure what you could say right now to make anything better, Roxie. But that's our problem, isn't it?"

She froze, trying to figure out what he meant by those words. Because that was the first time he'd ever actually talked about anything having to do with what was wrong between them. They were so good at tiptoeing around the issues and making sure the other was okay. But she loved him enough to let him go. Though, before she did that, she needed to make sure he was okay.

With those thoughts, she started to hate herself even more. And because of that, she knew that she truly needed to walk away. Because she wasn't sure she could like herself if this was the person she was becoming. A person who didn't speak and sank into herself. A person that was icy and cold. She didn't like that, and so, in order to make sure that didn't happen, she would ensure that the person, the thing that was causing the change within her, wasn't there anymore.

And that wasn't Carter.

It was her. It was Roxie when she was around Carter.

"Let me help you with your bandages since the nurses taught me how. And then we'll get you into bed."

"I'm not going upstairs, Roxie."

"I know."

He let out an awful breath. "Yeah, I guess I should be sleeping in the guest room anyway, right?" He didn't sound angry, didn't sound snide. The fact that there was a lack of emotion in his words cut even deeper.

But this was what she wanted, right? To let him go. To let him be the man he needed to be, so she could figure out the woman that she was.

Even if a little part of her broke, shattered into a thousand pieces, with every word that he spoke.

"It's on the first floor, so I figured it would be better for your leg while you're still healing."

"Are we just going to ignore the divorce papers sitting out on the table, mocking us?" He wasn't facing her, but he was looking directly at her in the mirror. She could see the stoniness of his expression, the darkness in his eyes. He didn't look angry, didn't appear sad. He just looked like the Carter she had seen for so long now. The one she couldn't read.

She didn't know if he was protecting himself or if he just didn't care.

She wasn't going to walk away when he was beaten down like this, though. Once he was strong, she would figure out the next step.

But they had to get there first.

"I don't know what you want me to say, Carter. It's not like it should be a surprise." She didn't know whose voice that was, the cool and collected, calm and almost icy one. That was not the Roxie she knew, but she couldn't stop it. It was like a defense mechanism, and she hated it.

"I see." His fingers tightened around the basin of the sink, and she almost reached out to put her hand on his back to soothe him like she used to. But she stopped herself. He didn't want her touch right then, and she wasn't sure if she could handle it either.

"Nothing's going to change right now, Carter. It

can't. You need to be healthy, you need to heal. And so, I'm going to help you with that."

"*Then* you're going to kick me out?"

She swallowed a breath.

"No, don't answer that. We don't need to talk about that. I'll get healthy, heal up as quickly as I can, and then I'll leave. You always loved this house, and I'm not going to stay in it if you don't want me here." Then he turned around and moved past her. He didn't even touch her as he walked through the doorway. She wondered why she wasn't crying. Wondered why it didn't hurt more.

Shouldn't it hurt when your heart was breaking? Shouldn't it hurt when everything you thought you knew was over?

Why wasn't she crying? Why couldn't she cry for her husband, the man that she thought she loved?

She'd cried for her sister, and Thea wasn't even as hurt as Carter was. She teared up at commercials and telephone calls that got to be too much. She shed tears at songs and memories.

But she couldn't cry when it mattered. She couldn't cry when he walked past her like she was a stranger. She couldn't cry when everything she thought she wanted was sifting through her fingertips.

Maybe there was a reason for that.

Maybe she had just told herself that this is what she wanted, and now that it wasn't working out the way it should have, her mind and heart just didn't care.

But it hurt, it hurt so much.

It pained her that there was something wrong with her, something deep down that she couldn't fix. And she didn't think staying here, staying past the time that Carter was healed would change that.

Because, no matter what, she was still going to hate herself in the end.

Maybe more than Carter hated her.

Carter got into bed, slowly, and with a pained look on his face. So, she moved closer to him and pulled the blankets back before helping him in. That forced her to put her hand on his side, and his shoulder. His body was so hot, the heat radiating from him and almost scorching her palm.

He was always fit, muscled yet lean. She'd always loved the way he looked, the way he felt when he was above her.

She had worshiped his body, much like he had worshiped hers, and it was hard remembering that she was walking away from this, leaving before he could.

He froze at her touch at first, and then let her help him into bed.

That was when she knew that he had to be hurting because he didn't let anyone help him.

He was so self-sufficient, so good at making sure everything he did was precise. He never let Roxie help him with anything, so the fact that he was letting her help him right then meant he was hurting.

Even though she didn't want to see him in pain, didn't want to even think about it, she'd never thought Carter was a man to give up.

No, that was all her.

She was the one giving up. Giving up before it hurt any more than it already did.

"Can I get you something to eat or drink, anything?"

He shook his head then winced. "Maybe some of my pain meds. I think I'm on the schedule for that, right?"

She nodded and then pulled out her phone so she could look at the timing. "You're right, we're actually a little bit past. That's why you're probably hurting as much as you are. Let me go get those for you. But don't you need something in your stomach for that?"

"I guess I do. I can go get it, though," Carter said as he tried to get back out of bed.

She put her hands on his shoulders, not really using any pressure, but he didn't fight her.

He never fought her.

Maybe that was the problem.

"I can get you some soup, and we have those crackers that you like. Just give me a few minutes. I have a protein shake for you too if you want to take that with your pills instead. That way, you can get something quick?"

"Sounds good to me." He wasn't looking at her, and she just wanted to break down right then. But like always, she didn't. She couldn't.

He looked like he wanted to say something, but he couldn't even look at her. Was it because he hated her or was it because of something else? She couldn't think of anything else it could possibly be, though. Not when she could see the look on his face. She couldn't read him, not like she needed to, but there was something different about him. Something that said that as soon as he could get out of this bed easily, it would be over.

And she wasn't going to break down because of that.

She couldn't let herself break down because of that.

And while part of her wanted to lean down and brush her lips over his forehead, she didn't.

So, she walked away and went to the kitchen. She just wanted to tell Carter something, let him know that everything would be okay, that she didn't want to leave him because she didn't want him anymore.

But telling someone to talk it out was easy. Actually talking it out was harder. And figuring out what to say meant figuring out that Roxie wasn't what he wanted. And she didn't think she could handle that.

So, she walked away, knowing that she would walk away again soon, and this time, she wouldn't be coming back.

That's when the tears fell. Slowly but surely, that's when she started to break.

But she wasn't broken yet.

CHAPTER THREE

Montgomery dinners had gone from awkward because he was the new guy, to a sense of home because they'd taken him in as one of their own.

Now, Carter wasn't sure what to make of them, he just knew that he wanted to be anywhere but sitting on the couch with the rest of them, trying not to stare. His body hurt. His head hurt even more from the effort it took to act like everything was normal. And he was pretty sure his heart was so numb at this point, he couldn't feel anything at all.

It had been almost a month since he was discharged, and while he was getting there in terms of his recovery, he still didn't have all the energy he needed to make it through the days without feeling as if he'd been run over by a truck.

He did his PT, and he had near-full range of movement, but he couldn't stand for eight hours a day and work. He couldn't do what he needed to do in order to pack up his things and leave before Roxie forced him out.

And he couldn't tell a damn soul that it was over. That the papers were ready to be signed, and all he had to do was leave his life's blood on the line, mix it with ink, and end what he'd thought was his future.

He'd spent almost a month in the guest room, not sleeping next to Roxie, not feeling her body along his, not sensing the heat of her as she slept. Before he'd moved down to the guest room after the accident, watching her sleep was the only way he saw her look relaxed. She was always so stressed out, and he used to think it had to do with her work. Over time, however, he figured it had to be because of him.

It had been a long month in which Carter had just tried to heal and figure out what the fuck he was going to do next. His body wasn't as badly damaged as he had feared, but his heart? His soul? That had taken one blow after another, and he was afraid he wouldn't like the man he became when he came out of it.

Now he sat on the couch, his leg propped up even

though he could put almost all of his weight on it now, but he had done what Roxie wanted because she had asked. She had looked at him with those wide eyes of hers and asked him to sit down and stay out of the way. So, he had.

Maybe she'd asked because she didn't want him to hurt himself, or perhaps it was because she didn't want to have to look at him when they were keeping so many secrets from the others.

Because from what he could tell, not a single person in this family, in this house, knew that she had asked him for a divorce.

No, that wasn't right. Roxie hadn't asked him. She had requested the divorce papers and didn't even have the decency to give them to him. But that wasn't really fair, was it? Not while they had shown up out of the blue. Maybe she'd had plans, ones that he just didn't know about. Regardless, it wasn't like he knew what the fuck he was doing. Everything was just so damn complicated, and he was tired. Tired of figuring out what she wanted, tired of figuring out what *he* wanted.

He just needed to heal, and then he would deal with things. He would take care of things much better than he had in the past because not doing so made things happen the way they did. Not dealing with things had put them in the position they were in right now.

"You're sitting here looking like hell warmed over," Mace said as he took a seat on the wooden coffee table near Carter.

"I thought the saying was death warmed over."

"True, but I try not to say *death* when it comes to you since you got so close." Mace winked as he said it, though Carter knew the other man had been worried. Hell, the whole family had been concerned. He didn't blame them since it had scared the shit out of him, too, but he was tired of being the invalid in the house.

"I wasn't that close," Carter argued. "And you'd rather say hell in the Montgomery house?

Mace snorted. "Well, have you met any of these people? Cursing is pretty much part of the normal language."

Carter shifted on the couch, a small smile playing on his face. "That is true." The Montgomerys were loud, brash, and caring. Somehow, they mixed all of that together and made it work. Made Carter miss the days when he actually had a family of his own. But Roxie was his family now...for however long he had her. That meant the Montgomerys were his, too. Though not for long.

Mace let out a breath. "The others are just in the kitchen getting things ready and talking. You can come in there, you know."

Carter shook his head. "No, I really can't."

"All you have to do is take the first step, Carter."

Carter knew Mace was talking about more than just walking into the kitchen. But the other man didn't know how everything had changed, how everything was going to shift even more as soon as Carter could stand on his feet for longer than an hour.

Because he was almost completely healed, even if he were lying down just then—mostly to appease Roxie. As soon as he was completely better, everything would change again. And he didn't think the Montgomerys were going to welcome him back with open arms after that. They weren't going to invite him back into the house as if he belonged there. Because Roxie was the reason he was allowed within these walls. They may take in strays with other non-family members, but that wasn't how Carter fit into this. He was Roxie's husband, and therefore, allowed to walk these hallowed halls.

But without Roxie? Carter would be on his own again. He was good at that. After all, other than his shop, he hadn't really had anything before he set eyes on Roxie Montgomery and had fallen hard and fast.

Probably too hard, and too fast.

But that was the problem with him, he never did

things in half measures. Apparently, Roxie was the same.

And now they were facing the consequences.

"Okay, are you allowed to have wine or beer with your meds?" Adrienne asked as she walked into the living room, a beer in one hand, a glass of wine in the other. She handed both over to Mace and winked. "If you can't have either, I'm sure Mace can take care of them both."

Mace rolled his eyes. "Thank you, dear woman. Or should I say *my* woman? I kind of like calling you my woman."

Adrienne narrowed her eyes at her fiancé. "You keep calling me your woman in that caveman tone, I might have to..." She paused, looking over at Carter before blushing. Adrienne never blushed, and Carter had a feeling that whatever she'd been about to say was something he didn't really want to hear.

"Never mind, I'm just going to walk away and..."

Carter held up his hands. "Don't walk away on my account. I'm just standing here, or rather laying here, wondering what's for dinner. And what you guys are all talking about. And I'll have that beer. I'm not on pain meds anymore." That had been both his decision and his doctor's. Hell, he was pretty much back to normal, but dreading the point where he'd be able to face himself in the mirror before he told Roxie that fact. "Mace can have the wine."

Mace handed over the beer, and Carter took a swig. "I'll have you know, I like wine." Mace sipped after he'd tilted his glass toward Carter in cheers. "Plus, the Montgomerys always have good wine."

"That is true. The Montgomerys do know how to put on a party."

Adrienne gave Carter a look, and he knew he was probably going to lose his mind soon. He didn't talk much, and when he did, he either grunted out words or rambled. Other than with Roxie, that was. When he was with her, he felt like he was himself. At least that's how it used to be. At first, she had intimidated him with her looks, her attitude, and just with the way she was. She was damned good at everything she did, except when it came to painting, but that was just a joke between the sisters.

But she was so good at everything that Carter sometimes felt like he was trying to catch up, like he wasn't good enough for her. But that had always been the case when it came to how he felt about Roxie. And he couldn't help the fact that sometimes his feelings were still in the way of everything. But there was no going back now. He couldn't.

The silence stretched, and Mace leaned toward

Adrienne. "So, what was that about me calling you woman? My woman?" Mace asked, his voice a growl. But he was smiling, so Carter knew that he was just putting on a show for him. Carter didn't mind, he was bored as fuck lying on this couch. He missed his job, even though he'd been back for a few days now, working in the office and getting caught up. His guys had kept the place running, but now he was in danger of being in the red if he didn't work his ass off. And that meant long hours.

Long hours once he was healthy. But that meant not being with Roxie.

Shit.

"I was going to say that if you call me your woman like that...maybe, you'd like it if I kicked you in the shin instead," Adrienne said, her voice sweet. A little too sweet.

"That's not what you were going to say."

"But it's what I'm saying now."

Adrienne turned to Carter, her blush high as she cleared her throat. "We can set you up in the kitchen if you want. You don't have to stay in here and wait for us to come back." She winced. "Roxie's up to her elbows in potatoes, or she would be out here I'm sure."

Carter knew that was a lie, but he wasn't going to correct Adrienne. "I'm just fine out here."

"No, you're not." Adrienne looked him right in the eyes then, and Carter just wanted to tell her that she should stop trying. Because Roxie had. And he wasn't going to cling to a family and an idea of a relationship that wasn't there anymore. It wasn't the fact that he had any self-respect, because he wasn't sure he did anymore. It was more the idea that he wasn't going to force himself into a life that didn't want him.

And if it didn't want him, then he wasn't sure he would like himself if he tried to stay.

"Okay, dears, dinner's almost ready, and we are going to move you into the dining room," Mrs. Montgomery said as she hurried into the living room.

Carter had always loved Roxie's parents. They were welcoming and open. Yes, they always wanted to know more about him, even if it was a little prying at times, but he had married their baby girl, and that meant he had to deal with the interrogations. It didn't mean that he was going to tell them everything, though. There really wasn't much to say.

He was just Carter Marshall. Orphan, all alone in a big world of seemingly endless Montgomerys, and about to walk away from their daughter because she wanted it. He wasn't going to stay where he wasn't wanted. Had never stayed, even in the days where it would've been easier to do so.

So, he may not hate himself in the morning, but he may hate himself later.

"I can get there on my own," Carter said, keeping his voice light. "I was just enjoying this couch here a little too much." He tried to smile as he said it, but he knew from the way that Mace looked at him that it hadn't reached his eyes.

Carter was in a shitty mood, and it was just going to get worse as he finished up healing and waited to take that next step where he walked away from everything. But he couldn't really blame Roxie for delivering the papers, could he? Because they had walked away from each other emotionally long before this. The physical paperwork was just a formality at this point.

"Well, if you say so, but we're still going to move you into the dining room. Because Roxie's mashed potatoes are almost done, and my roast is exquisite."

Carter smiled then, his mouth watering. "I sure do love your roasts. My favorite thing that you make."

He was going to miss it when he couldn't get it anymore.

He was going to miss a lot of things.

"Oh, I know it's your favorite, that's why I made it today. It's your first Montgomery dinner since everything happened. And it's about time you get everything you want."

Mace helped Carter up from the couch so he could get to his walker. He didn't really need it at this point because he was almost finished healing, but it made everyone feel better when he used it. "Thanks, Mrs. Montgomery."

He thought about her words as he slowly trudged his way to the dining room. Everything he wanted? He already had that.

But now he was going to lose it.

No, he'd already lost it.

Because he was a fucking idiot.

He'd lost it even though he didn't know how he ever had it in the first place. Lost it because he wasn't sure that he was strong enough to hold onto it.

He had thought they were on rocky ground before, but as he took his seat at the table, Roxie taking the chair next to him because that was where she always sat, and sitting anywhere else would just put a big red flag on their failing relationship, Carter wondered why it hurt so much.

Was it really supposed to hurt like this?

He had known something like this was coming for months now. They had just started to drift apart to the point where he wasn't even sure who Roxie and Carter were anymore. Seeing that it wasn't truly that big of a surprise, why did it hurt so much?

But it *had* been a surprise.

Even though it shouldn't have been, it was.

As soon as he saw those papers, he felt as if he'd been kicked in the gut. Everything had just gone black and dim for a moment as he fought to catch his breath. It hadn't been the pain of everything happening, it had just been the fact that he was losing her.

And those papers solidified it.

"Can you pass the rolls?" Dimitri asked, bringing Carter out of his thoughts.

Everybody was sitting at the dinner table passing around food and talking about their days. The kids were at the table, too, smiling and laughing and giggling with one another. And Dimitri's dog, Captain, was sitting by his master's side, sweetly looking up at the table, hoping for food. Not that the dog actually ate people-food, but the Golden liked to pretend that he was in dire need of it.

Everybody was here. A great big family. And Roxie hadn't said a fucking word to him yet.

Not that he could talk to her either.

"So, do you really need the walker now?" Shep asked, a frown on his face. "'Because you were walking just fine earlier."

"I'm fine without it," Carter said, ignoring the way

he could feel Roxie's eyes glaring at him. Maybe not glaring, but shooting daggers for sure.

"Then why are you using it?" Roxie's brother asked, still piling potatoes onto his plate.

"They gave it to me after the first checkup just in case my leg gave out. It hasn't yet, though. It's mostly just to make sure all of you guys realize that I'm doing okay, or at least I think."

"The doctor said you should use it, so that's why you have it," Roxie said. It was the first thing she had said to him all fucking day. They had spent all day together in that house of theirs, in the echoing chamber of everything they once had, and she hadn't said a word to him. She had just calmly and silently helped him around the house, even when he didn't need the help.

To say that the marriage was well and truly over was probably an understatement at this point.

"Well, I'm glad that you're getting better, even if the walker is really just for show at this point. I hope." Thea sat next to him and patted his hand, her eyes bright. The two of them hadn't really talked much since everything happened, but she had been dealing with so much of her own stuff for the past month or so, he didn't really blame her. Plus, he had a feeling that she didn't really want to come over to the house to thank him or whatever she needed to do to make herself feel better about what had happened, not when she had to know what was going on and was standing between Roxie and himself. Roxie was Thea's sister so, of course, Thea needed to take her sister's side. Carter just hated that there were sides at all.

It wasn't like he was waiting for a thank you. He didn't need gratitude for pushing Thea out of the way. Yeah, he had gotten hurt, but anyone would've done it.

The hope and gratefulness in their eyes when they looked at him just made him sick.

Because it wasn't real. It couldn't be. Not when everything was going to end any day now.

They continued their dinner, talking about random things and letting him be quiet for the rest of the evening. He didn't miss the fact that Roxie didn't speak either. It was just so damned awkward between them now, and he hated it. But it wasn't like he could change things. Not when she had asked for the divorce. And he was probably going to let it happen.

By the time they got home, Carter was exhausted and not because of his body, because his brain and his heart hurt. They were heavy, filled to the brim with everything that he didn't need and yet everything that pushed at him.

They stood in the entryway, Roxie near the stairs so she could go up to the master bedroom that he didn't share with her anymore, and him facing the guest room where he would be sleeping for the rest of his time under this roof.

"Can I help you with anything before bed?" Roxie asked, her voice hollow. He couldn't tell what she was thinking, didn't know what she was feeling.

But that was the problem, wasn't it?

"I'm fine, goodnight."

They still had a couple of hours before bed, but neither of them commented on that. They were just going to go their separate ways, a prelude to what would happen as soon as Carter was completely healed.

Roxie gave him a tight nod and then went upstairs. He did his best not to look at her. Because when he looked at her, he ached.

Because he missed his wife. He missed her smile, he missed everything about her.

He missed the way she would laugh at something inane and then bury her face in her hands because she knew that it was silly to laugh at it.

He missed her touch, her taste. Yeah, he missed sex, but it wasn't like they'd had sex recently. They used to have their hands on each other all the time.

And then she'd stopped talking.

She'd stopped smiling.

And he couldn't figure out how to make her do either of them again. He'd tried, but it hadn't worked.

And then, eventually, he'd stopped trying altogether.

And she hadn't done anything about it.

So, this was his fault. Because he had tried, and he'd failed. It would always be his fault.

Always.

CHAPTER FOUR

Brushes with Lushes was the tradition, a routine, something that Roxie and her friends and family loved to do once a month. Brushes with Lushes was something that she secretly despised, but only because she wasn't really good at it. Oh, the lush part, the part where you drank wine while you pretended to paint, that part she was pretty good at. It was the brushes part, the one where she actually had to be an artist. That part, she wasn't very good at.

The fact that the rest of her family seemed to be full of artists probably had something to do with why she felt so inadequate when it came to the brushes part of Brushes with Lushes.

Brushes with Lushes—man did she hate saying that name in her head forty times, but she did because she would likely mess it up one day—was run by Kaylee, their newer friend, but one who had become close over time. At least close to the others in Roxie's family. She didn't know Kaylee that well, and she kind of regretted that. It was mostly because Roxie was so far into her own mind and her own problems lately, she'd pretty much pushed a lot of people out to make room.

She hated feeling selfish, but that was apparently all her brain could do these days.

Because in order for Roxie to focus on her work, her life, and the fact that everything was crumbling around her, she had to keep from thinking about other things.

And that meant that she had no idea what was going on with Shea and Shep. The fact that they had moved up with their daughter Livvy from New Orleans a little over a year ago meant that Roxie should have been closer to her brother and his family. But, in reality, she sometimes felt as if she were closer to them when they were just using Skype and making phone calls. Hell, she had probably been closer to Shep when she was just writing him letters when he first moved away to find his art and himself. Now, he was back—a husband, a father, and far more settled than he had ever been when he first left Colorado for New Orleans.

But she didn't really know what the couple was up to. She didn't know if Livvy was enjoying her new home. Didn't know if Shea liked living in a new place. Yes, the woman worked in the same field as Roxie, but that didn't mean they actually worked together. She didn't know anything because she hadn't asked. Because she was so self-absorbed lately, she hadn't been able to. And she hated herself for that. But the main thing was, if she asked, she knew they would ask about her and Carter. And Roxie wasn't ready to talk about that. Not yet. Maybe not ever.

She didn't even know if her brother and sister-in-law were going to have another baby. She ignored the twinge that always came when she thought those words, about what would happen if Shea got pregnant again, and just focused on walking through the doorway of the studio where Brushes with Lushes was held.

And then she saw Abby sitting next to Shea, and she winced. Roxie hadn't even known that Abby had found love again with a tattoo artist, one of the Montgomerys' friends named Ryan. She didn't know anything about their relationship because she had been so focused on getting Carter better and not talking about what was important.

Abby and Ryan was apparently a very new relationship, but the two were head-over-heels in love with each other.

And Roxie really tried not to feel nervous about that. Because anything that burned that hot and that fast wasn't necessarily doomed to fizzle out, but considering what she was living with right then, Roxie couldn't help but hope that Ryan and Abby's relationship didn't end up like hers and Carter's. Especially for Abby's daughter's sake. Julia didn't need to lose another man in her life. Although Roxie knew that Julia had never met her father because he had passed away when Abby was still pregnant, the little girl didn't need any more loss.

None of them did.

Roxie took a seat next to Abby and gave the other woman a small smile before she looked to her right. She tried to keep that smile up for her two sisters. Thea and Adrienne watched her like hawks, maybe not necessarily waiting for her to break down and feel weak, but at least looking to see when Roxie might finally speak to them.

She just wasn't ready yet. And, yes, that was selfish, but that was who Roxie was. Selfish, cool, and evil. At least that's what she kept telling herself as she wondered why she couldn't fix what was going on with her and Carter. But sometimes there was nothing to fix. Sometimes, it was just better to walk away before somebody got hurt even more.

"I was wondering if you were going to show up," Thea said, a patient smile on her face. "You're usually never this late."

Roxie winced and put her bag under the table. "Sorry. The office ran late, and then I needed to go home and change so I wasn't coming here in a suit." She'd been home for all of twenty minutes, ten of those spent standing outside of Carter's door, wondering what she could say, wondering if she could speak to him at all.

She hadn't knocked.

Hadn't wanted to bother him.

"You do look cute in that suit, though," Adrienne said, her eyes imploring. Adrienne wasn't a gossip, wasn't too probing, but both of Roxie's sisters truly wanted to help her. She knew that. She just didn't want to ask for help. She didn't want to mess things up more than she already had. And in order to make that happen, she needed to fix everything herself and then come to her sisters for the final parts where they could smooth everything over.

It all sounded so idiotic when she said it to herself, but she *was* an idiot.

Roxie smiled a little bit more this time, hoping it didn't look brittle. "Well, I know I look great in a suit. Thankfully, I do, because it's sort of part of my job."

"Don't I know it. Although I think Shep really likes me in a suit. After all, the suit and the bun at the back of my head were pretty much what drew him to me." Shea grinned, and the rest of them laughed. Shea had gone in for a tattoo down in New Orleans, and that was how she had met Shep. Apparently, she had been a little icier then, a little more reserved than she was now. But the two of them were it for each other. Shea brought out the calmness in Shep, and he brought out the warmth in her.

Roxie hadn't known Shea before she got with Shep, but from what the couple had said, they had both come out of their shells exactly as they needed to. They were exactly who they needed to be for themselves and each other.

And Roxie was only a little bit envious of that. Because, after all, she had thought Carter was exactly who she needed. The one who could bring her out of her shell. The one who could help her stand on her own two feet. Because she wasn't always good at that.

Her family was so talented, so full of depth and honor. There was Shep, the older and wiser one, who had always been the life of the party, even when he was the responsible one. He was one of the best tattoo artists in the country, only fighting for the top position in competition with the rest of her family it seemed.

Adrienne was another of those top tattoo artists. Plus, she always seemed to have everything handled, even when she felt like she was failing. She had opened up her own business with Shep, and it was thriving. And Adrienne always had a new hobby, not letting the other go because she couldn't do it, but because she had mastered it and wanted to learn something else. First, it had been knitting, and then singing, then back to knitting, and now she was doing much better at this whole painting thing than Roxie could ever hope to do. Considering that Adrienne was an artist, albeit with ink on skin as canvas rather than what they were painting on now, it made sense.

But, apparently, Adrienne was starting to paint on her own, even setting up a little studio at her house. Roxie hadn't seen it yet, but she would. As soon as she got her head out of her ass and started being part of the Montgomerys again.

And then there was Thea. Perfect Thea. God, Roxie hated how that sounded in her head. Because she was not jealous of her sister. She adored her sibling and loved the fact that Thea was everything. She was an amazing businesswoman, an entrepreneur, the best baker in the history of bakers in Roxie's opinion. Although Thea wouldn't say that. She was amazing at what she did, and soon, her business, Colorado Icing, would expand even more. She put her all into everything and was now finally in love with the man she probably should have been in love with from the start. All of Roxie's family and friends were falling in love it seemed, and she couldn't help but wonder where she had gone wrong.

Because she loved Carter, loved the idea of him.

But she didn't love how being with him made her feel these days.

She didn't love the fact that she was so in her head that she was missing out on the rest of her life.

So, she just needed to breathe. And take things one day at a time.

Even if it didn't make sense to anyone else.

Kaylee walked into the room at that moment, brandishing a nice bottle of rosé.

The other woman grinned as she set down the bottle on the front table. "This is my reward for finishing my painting in the room, though I won't taste a sip until you're all ready for me to critique your work." She laughed as she said it, and the others joined her.

Roxie couldn't help the turn of her stomach at the word *critique*. Kaylee didn't actually judge their paintings since the class was more about community and friendship than putting out art that could sell. But knowing that didn't make her feel any better about it.

Because Roxie really wasn't that good at this whole thing. She tried to be. She hadn't yet resorted to taking private lessons on the side so she could at least paint a somewhat straight line, but she had thought about it. If she weren't so busy during tax season and with learning about what was going on between her and Carter, she might have been able to actually take some time to learn how to draw. Because even though Thea didn't technically think of herself as an artist, she was. Between decorating cakes and cookies, her sister was amazingly talented when it came to art. Abby and Shea were also pretty decent at it, though none of them compared to Adrienne's talent.

Not that anybody actually compared themselves. Only Roxie did that. And that was because she *wasn't* good at it. And she hated not being good at things.

She was good, sometimes even great, at everything she tried most times—because she attempted as many things as Adrienne did—but, sometimes, like with art, she just wasn't.

And she hated failing.

The fact that she was doing her best not to correlate that she hated failing at art with the fact that she was failing at her marriage wasn't lost on her. But she was not going to think about that. Because the more she thought about it, the worse her art got, and the more she wanted to get into the lushes part of Brushes with Lushes.

"Okay, ladies. Today, we're working on a moonscape. I know, you're so surprised. Brushes with Lushes working on moonscapes… But, I know that you all love moons and trees, and it's still quite dark and cold outside. So, it was either this or a forestscape with just snow. Maybe next time we'll go with bright colors and palm trees in the Caribbean so we can imagine that we're somewhere in warm weather." Kaylee laughed with the rest of the group, and Roxie just shook her head, a smile playing on her face.

She really liked Kaylee and had heard through the grapevine that the other woman may or may not be seeing another member of their group. A man named Landon. Roxie didn't really know Landon well, though her sisters did. It seemed that everybody was finding love and lust these days. Everybody but Roxie.

But she wasn't going to think about that right then.

Because if she did, she would get depressed, or even *more* depressed than she already was. And then her sisters would try not to ask even more questions. Because they were giving her space. But by giving her space, it was making her feel like she was being closed in. She had no idea how that worked, but they were being so careful around her, that she was having trouble remembering exactly who she was supposed to be. Remembering exactly how she was supposed to act so it didn't look like her whole life was falling apart.

"We can totally do this," Shea said, grinning. "Right?"

"I think I'm going to need more wine." Roxie did her best to look like she was joking, but she still took a very large sip of her drink. She might need to call a car service to get back home if tonight continued as it was.

"Moons I can do. It's how they reflect light on everything else that I can't do," Thea said, her teeth worrying her lip.

"But Kaylee is going to show us how to do that, right?" Roxie asked, suddenly worried that she was standing in front of a blank canvas. A blank canvas that not only represented the art that she didn't know how to do but also the future and what would happen once Carter was completely healed. Because Carter was better. He could work now. Maybe not as many hours as he used to, but that hadn't been healthy for either of them. Everything was going to change, and Roxie's life mirrored this blank canvas.

Maybe she'd already had too much wine if this was where her mind was going before she'd even put a single brush stroke on the page. It didn't matter that it had been one very big gulp of wine. She was drunk on adrenaline and worry. Drunk on a future that she was afraid wouldn't come.

Or maybe it was coming at her too fast, and she couldn't catch her breath.

"We're going to be fine. Just one stroke at a time." Abby was looking toward the front as she spoke, her attention on Kaylee as their instructor started the evening with a single brush stroke. And just like that, the canvas wasn't blank anymore. It was the start of something. The start of art? The start of the end? Or just a beginning.

It wasn't empty.

It was *something*.

And Roxie needed to remember that.

The group worked together, laughing, and Roxie was able to somewhat forget her worries. It was easier to do when she was focused on trying to be better at something, something that had nothing to do with her marriage. Plus, she really just enjoyed spending time with her family and friends. It was easier to spend time with them when they weren't asking questions, when they weren't looking at her with pitying looks in their eyes, wondering what was going on between her and her husband. It wasn't their fault that she was failing at most things these days. It wasn't their fault that they wanted to help. But she didn't even know how to ask for help. What was it that she could actually ask them anyway? Because it didn't make any sense for her to want to ask them anything. They had their own lives. They were succeeding, where Roxie was failing. And bothering them with something that they couldn't help with wouldn't aid anyone.

So, Roxie had her one glass of wine and hung out with her friends and her family. She tried to pretend that everything was okay in the world. In the end, her art wasn't that bad. It wasn't good, but no one made fun of her for it. Hell, no one ever made fun of her art. Because that wasn't what Brushes with Lushes was about. It didn't matter that Roxie was competitive and hated failing. It didn't matter that she had been the one to put all of that weight on her shoulders. It still felt like she should be able to do something better than she was.

Kaylee came over at the end and gave Roxie a hug.

"You did so well, honey." The woman squeezed her again, and Roxie just gave her a smile.

"Thank you for pretending."

"I wouldn't tell you a lie. You know that, above all else. I may point you in another direction, but I would never tell you a lie. You're getting better—not that you weren't great to begin with. And that is not a lie, so don't roll your eyes at me. Just because you paint differently than your sisters and aren't a savant like I am,"—she rolled her eyes this time, and Roxie laughed—"does not mean that you are not an artist. An artist isn't what they produce, it's how they produce it. It's how they feel when they do it. And, most artists hate what they're doing as they're doing it. In my opinion, that's what makes good art. The loathing. The betrayal." This time, everybody laughed with Kaylee, and Roxie just snorted.

"Overdramatic much?"

Kaylee just narrowed her eyes at Roxie. "We can discuss overdramatic later, can't we?"

"Ouch." Now that hurt. Because, yes, Roxie tended to be overdramatic, but mostly just in her head. Although she had a feeling that Kaylee could read minds. She didn't know why, but the other woman always knew exactly when Roxie was in a bout of self-loathing. Even her sisters couldn't figure that out. Mostly, they just thought that she was stressed out about something. But Kaylee always knew exactly when Roxie was freaking out about something stupid. Or maybe freaking out about something so important she wanted to *make* it stupid.

"On that note, I am heading home. You guys have a great night."

They all hugged and kissed and promised they

would see each other soon. And they would. They were all pretty close, some closer than others since Roxie had been pulling away for the past year. She had to do better, had to stop hiding from herself. And she would do that. After.

Everything was after.

She just had to deal with the fact that her marriage was failing. No, she had to deal with the fact that her marriage had failed.

When she got home, Carter was in his room, the door closed.

His room. Not the guest room. *His* room. It had only been a month, yet that's what she thought. The fact that it was his room. They didn't share a room anymore. They didn't share anything anymore.

And he was better. He was so much better. He'd gone to work that day, like he had all week. Carter was mostly in the office, so that meant that he was working hours again, just not overdoing it. At least, according to Dimitri. Because she hadn't asked. And Carter hadn't offered the information. But him being better and working meant that he would leave soon. Or maybe she would. She didn't need this house, didn't need the memories of what could have been, and of what she'd let slip through her fingers. But she had a feeling that Carter would be the one to walk away. Because he was proud. But then again, so was she.

But things would change soon. The anvil was ready to fall.

And they would walk away from each other.

Because he didn't love her. Maybe he never loved her.

And she couldn't force him to be with her.

Not anymore.

CHAPTER FIVE

He'd never hated the idea that he was fine any more than he did just then. Carter didn't want to be fine. He didn't want his body to be fully healed. Because now that he could move, now that he knew he could work the long hours that he needed to, everything was going to change.

The problem was that it had already changed. It'd changed so quickly that Carter hadn't been able to catch up, or even hold on for dear life with his knuckles going white, his fingers clinging to the shreds of what he and Roxie had had.

But now, he was healed.

And he needed to do what was right.

His doctor had cleared him, and now he sat on his

bed in the guest room that wasn't a guest room anymore and put his head in his hands.

It was time.

Putting off the inevitable would only hurt them both, and he was just so damn tired. So damn tired of waiting for the end to come when it was already there.

Valentine's Day was in three weeks, a day that most people said was all marketing, all love and hearts and chocolate and cards, but that day did symbolize something for him and Roxie. It reminded them that what they had was probably gone because the paperwork was out, and they weren't talking.

Roxie didn't want to speak to him, and he didn't know how to make her talk.

He didn't want to wait any longer—until she told him to leave.

Because the paperwork might mean that, but she still hadn't said the words. So, he would do it for them both. Because he wasn't going to stay for another three weeks and wait until that holiday arrived. Wait until that day came where they had to look at one another and realize that maybe love wasn't enough.

He rolled his eyes, annoyed with himself for thinking that. But maybe it was the truth. Maybe love *wasn't* enough. Because relationships took hard work and communication, and even if he and Roxie had all of that—which they had at first—it wasn't enough.

Lust and aching and everything that came with actually living...that made things hard.

And even though life was hard, and Carter damn well knew that, sometimes, making things easier for those you cared about was all that mattered. Because he didn't want Roxie to hate him, and he didn't want to start hating her. And waiting until Valentine's Day, until the day filled with love and happiness and all that crap wouldn't work. He knew he couldn't do it.

He let out a sigh and stood up, taking a look around the room that had become his after coming home from the hospital. The only time he'd gone upstairs recently was when Roxie wasn't at the house, and he needed to get a few things from the master.

The thing was, though, most of his clothes and other stuff was down here now. He didn't own much, and frankly, neither did Roxie, but what Carter had, was mostly with him now. So, it was depressingly easy to pack it all up into a couple of duffels and set them by the end of the bed.

He'd come back for more—or maybe he wouldn't. Perhaps he'd leave it all here. Just like he'd leave most of himself.

Jesus Christ, he didn't want to go. Didn't want to walk away from what he thought he wanted. But, the thing was, *he* wasn't wanted.

And he didn't want to stay where he would be in the way.

Roxie wanted a divorce.

So, he'd give her one.

He let out a breath and picked up his bags, thankful that his body didn't ache, and the scars on his legs didn't pull too badly. Of course, the wounds on his heart hurt like hell, but he was going to ignore those and not think about what might happen next.

He would give Roxie what she wanted, what she needed, and he'd figure out what to do with the rest of his life.

He'd married the woman he loved. Married her because of circumstances that had put them together, but also because he wanted her in his life. When what they'd thought they had changed, he'd tried to hold on.

It hadn't worked.

And now it was time to deal with the consequences of those actions.

Roxie would be home any minute from work because she'd been bringing her work home with her these days. Yes, she worked late hours since it was tax season, and this was always her busiest set of months, but instead of working at the office until she missed dinner like she usually did, she'd been coming home.

For him.

He might have thought that was a sign that maybe they could work things out, but she was so closed off from him—and if he were honest with himself, he was just as closed off from her—that he didn't think it was truly a sign at all.

Carter walked out of the house, careful not to look at anything too closely on the way or he'd get distracted, and she'd see the bags first before he could explain about his plans. Yes, he might have seen the papers first before she had a chance to tell him about them, but he wouldn't do the same to her. Now that he wasn't gut-punched, he could think clearly and know that she hadn't let him find out that way on purpose.

The two of them didn't hurt one another like that. That wasn't their thing.

The problem was, they didn't *have* a thing. Not anymore.

That was one of their problems anyway. Honestly, they had too many to count, and they all revolved around the one subject they *didn't* talk about. The thing that neither of them wanted to mention.

And because Carter's stomach hurt just thinking about it, he pushed those thoughts away like he always did and put his bags into the cab of his truck before she got home. He'd talk to her in the house where she would feel safe and not have the evidence of his leaving thrust in her face. Not to mention, he'd need an easy exit, and him putting on a show of gathering his belongings would just prolong the inevitable pain that he knew would rip through him when he closed that door behind him for the final time.

He couldn't believe it had come to this. It *shouldn't* have come to this. And yet he had no idea what he was supposed to do about it. Roxie wanted a divorce, had wanted it for some time if her actions were any indication. Now, he was just going to have to find a way to move on.

Find a way to move forward and not get sick or lose himself in the end.

Carter walked back into the house and stuffed his hands into the pockets of his jeans. He was going to miss this place, even with the memories of the silence and aching looks and fears of what to do next. Roxie had bought the house before she met him and had already been living here by the time they got engaged. She hadn't fully decorated it until he moved in because she'd been busy with work and had said that she didn't like not knowing what to do to make it look the way she wanted.

She always put herself down when it came to art or what she perceived was her sisters' and brother's area of talent. He'd tried to stop that, had tried to tell her that she had depth and talent in those areas as well, but she hadn't taken his words to heart. Or maybe she was so deep into thinking she couldn't do certain things that nothing he said would have made it better. He'd tried to show her how talented she was in how they made the place their own, but he didn't think it had stuck.

The fact that she tortured herself with Brushes with Lushes like she did just told Carter that she was going to try her best to find talent where she didn't think she had any. The thing was, though, she *did* have talent. In so many damn things. But she refused to see it.

And Carter hadn't known how to help her do that.

And now he was going to leave, and he wouldn't be able to even try anymore.

Why did that thought hurt more than it should?

The door opened behind him, and he turned on his heel to see Roxie standing there, her eyes wide and her bag in her hand. She looked so damn pretty. Always did, and he knew she always would. Her dark hair was pulled back into a bun thing that he thought she called a chignon or something. She had on makeup that appeared natural, but he knew she took time to make it come across that way. He loved the way she looked with it and without it. She had a way to make her eyes pop, her lips do the same. But he also loved when she was freshly scrubbed and all dewy. Or when she was up too late and telling him that she felt like garbage. He loved the way she looked then, too.

He just loved her.

This was going to hurt far more than the burns on his legs.

"Carter? Is everything okay? I didn't expect you to be standing right there when I walked in." She cleared her throat, closed the door behind her, and set her bag on the table in the entryway. The same table where he'd first seen the papers. The one they'd bought together at a flea market and had tried to sand and make look professional. It was a sad state of what they could do and it had worn down in places that were now covered up by antique-looking lanterns. If they put too much weight on it, it wobbled, and he was pretty sure one of the metal parts on the bottom wasn't attached correctly.

But it was theirs. Something they had built together. And something that was a pretty damn good symbol of who they were, wasn't it?

He was the one that cleared his throat. "Roxie."

She blinked, clasping her hands in front of her, a

shield that she brandished when she was nervous. One that she put up against him.

He hated this.

Hated himself.

But it needed to be done.

"I'm all healed, Rox. The doctor gave me the go-ahead to go back to my normal hours at the shop, and my PT is still going, but I'm doing okay health-wise."

She nodded. "You've been doing so well."

He nodded back, feeling awkward as hell. His hands were still in his pockets, safe there so he didn't reach out and try to touch her. He missed the feel of her skin, missed the way she used to lean into him when he cupped her face.

But he couldn't do that. Not anymore. And he had to be the stronger person in order to make sure that happened. Because if he took a step toward her, he'd break when she stepped away. Because they weren't who they needed to be. He wasn't the man she needed. Not anymore. Maybe not ever.

"I don't know what to do next, Rox. And because of that, I'm going to go. I'll sign the papers when the time comes." His mouth went dry, his hands turning sweaty. "I'm going to go," he repeated. "This was your house first, Roxie. I'm not going to take it from you. I'll be at

Landon's for a bit, and then I'll figure out where to go next."

He looked into her eyes then, willing her to speak, hoping she'd tell him not to leave. But she didn't. She didn't say a damn thing, and he knew he was lost. All was lost. And he had no idea what the fuck to do next.

"I have a couple bags in the truck, and I'll probably be back for more soon. Or whatever. I don't know. But I'm going to go." He kept saying those words. He hated them.

"Whatever you need, Carter." Her voice was so calm, so smooth.

Why couldn't she break like he was?

Then again, he really wasn't breaking, was he? If he were, he'd have told her that he didn't want to leave, that he wanted to stay and work this out. But he didn't know what there was left of them to work out.

Jesus Christ, he was leaving his wife.

Leaving because she'd taken the first step with those papers.

And he wasn't going to stay and make her hurt. Wasn't going to remain and make himself do the same.

"I guess...I guess we'll talk soon."

She gave him a tight nod before she finally took a step to the side, then another. Moving out of his way so he could make it to the door. Moving so he could leave.

Neither of them fought.

Why weren't they fighting?

He made his way to the door, pausing right beside her. They stood next to each other, him facing the door, and her facing the rest of the house, but neither of them faced the other.

"I..." He couldn't finish the sentence, didn't know what to say.

"I'm sorry," she whispered and then she walked away, her steps quick as she practically ran upstairs.

And he let her go. Because she was *sorry*.

And the thing was, so was he.

It was just too late for either of them to do anything about it.

So, he walked out the door, made his way to his truck, and left the house he'd finally found a home in. Left the wife he loved yet didn't know if she loved him back. Left the life he'd thought he made.

Left it all because she'd asked.

Left it all because he was afraid there was nothing left.

Left it.

And she was...sorry.

Carter wiped the tear running down his face and drove away, knowing it was over. Knowing he hadn't fought the good fight because he hadn't known how to start it.

He'd regret this.

He knew it.

He'd regret this.

And he'd break.

The first fracture was already there.

The next was on its way.

CHAPTER SIX

Pain stabbed through Roxie's side, but she pushed through, focusing on her breathing and the burning in her legs rather than her lungs. She just had to remember that she enjoyed this sort of thing—or was learning to enjoy it.

She used to cross-country ski when she was in high school and then into college, but had promptly quit when she got a job and put her all into her work. That meant it had been more than a few years since she'd been on skis, and her body was punishing her for it.

She let out a breath, moving her arms and legs in a tempo she could sustain for the rest of this uphill climb, all the while thinking that she was going to love the downhill part since that meant less burning in her lungs. At least, theoretically.

She'd joined the weekend team a month ago and hadn't looked back. She worked five days a week, ten to twelve hours a day, and on weekends when she wasn't burying herself in paperwork, she was out here on the mountain. She'd lived in Colorado all her life and realized she had taken the mountains and their beauty for granted.

She'd taken a lot for granted it seemed.

No, she wasn't going to think about that. She didn't want to think about anything that would pull her focus from her training and the fun she had while doing something for herself. So, she moved into her breathing and made her way to the top of the hill, the others at her side or in front of her.

She wasn't the fastest at this, and frankly, she was probably the slowest one out here, but that was fine by her. Oddly fine, in fact. Because they'd had years of training, and she was just getting back into it. She didn't have to compete with them, only herself. And for someone who had to compete with everything, including her family when it came to hobbies for freak's sake, she counted that as growth.

It probably helped that she'd sunk into herself and had only been thinking about work and cross-country skiing for the past month. She'd ignored calls, emails, texts, and people coming over who were trying to soothe her when all she wanted to do was ignore the world and try to find something that she could actually do without failing.

If it took freezing temperatures, snow all around her, and burning lungs and muscles to do that, then she'd take it.

Because she was so damn scared of what would happen when she no longer focused on the hill in front of her and instead locked on the ones behind her—waiting, always waiting.

Roxie pushed again, enjoying the cool wind on her face and the fact that it sort of burned, just not the same type of burn the rest of her experienced. She was going to hurt tomorrow, that much she knew, but it would be worth it. Because she was doing okay. She would be okay. Because she had to be.

She looked to her right and smiled at the man next to her. She couldn't see his eyes since both of them were wearing dark sunglasses, but she had a feeling he winked. Liam always winked. He liked pretending that everything was fine, just like she feigned. That was why they got along. He was the reason she was even on this team, the reason she had been able to find this place—and maybe try to find a part of herself again.

He was the only family member that she saw with regularity these days, Liam Montgomery, her cousin from Boulder. He drove over an hour south to come down here and cross-country ski with her, even though he had a cabin up in the woods near Boulder, and there were closer places for him to work out like this. There were other teams that would probably work better for him, too.

But he came down here for her and hadn't said a word to her about the fact that her marriage was over or that Carter had left a month ago. He hadn't asked her how she was doing, hadn't asked her if she had spoken to her husband.

She hadn't.

Liam hadn't asked her anything, just said that he was joining a new team up in the mountains near her and that every Saturday and Sunday he would be out here doing something that she used to do and love. He hadn't even invited her, had just said that was what he would be doing. And she had shown up.

And so now she and her cousin were part of this cross-country team that wasn't really a team but rather a group of people who did something they liked to do and were decently good at. Nobody was going to be joining the Olympic team, or even trying out for medals. A lot of them had former injuries or weren't really athletes. Not in the strictest sense of the word anyway. But they were all enjoying it, and the weather had been cooperating for the last month for this to happen. Roxie was actually surprised that it had considering the time of year it was. She didn't want to think about Valentine's Day and how it had gone...or rather, how she'd ignored it with everything she had.

She was just going up this next hill, and then down the other side, and then she'd head to her car. Because she was exhausted and really just wanted to go home.

But that wasn't even really the case, was it? She didn't want to go home. She hated her home. She hated the fact that the walls seemed to talk to her, even as they were completely still and silent. She swore she could hear Carter's voice, could hear his laughter, and she hated it. She didn't hate his voice, didn't hate his laugh, she just hated that they weren't there anymore. She hated that every time she turned around, she saw something that was Carter, something that reminded her of what they used to have. Something that reminded her that he wasn't there anymore.

She had been the one to request the papers. She was the one who started this.

But *he* had left.

She didn't know why she hated herself for that. Didn't know why she hated him at the same time. It didn't make any sense. Because they'd both made choices. Why did Roxie feel like she needed to blame somebody for it?

But that was life. That was hearts. And nothing made sense now that everything had changed around her.

Roxie turned away from Liam then and made her way up the hill and then down the back side. By the time they were all at their cars, laughing and joking, drinking their hot cocoa or coffee and their buckets of water at this point, she didn't know what to say. She never really knew what to say with this group of people. No one really knew her outside of being Liam's cousin and a woman that wanted to learn how to cross-country ski again. They didn't know her past, they didn't know that she was an accountant and worked long hours. They didn't know that she was the youngest of four, or that there were so many Montgomery cousins that it was a little ridiculous. They didn't know that her husband had left her. They didn't know any of that. So, there was no pity in their eyes, though there *were* some questions.

But nobody really asked them. Nobody really asked anybody anything. It was as if every single person on this team had secrets and they didn't want to venture out and see exactly what the others were hiding. And Roxie was just fine with that. Being in a group of people that didn't feel sorry for her because she was alone was actually quite refreshing. It helped her not think about the fact that she was alone.

And, yes, she needed to think about that. She needed to actually give Carter the papers and have him sign them.

She needed to sign them herself.

She needed to talk to Carter and figure out what they were going to do with the house and all of their stuff.

Because it wasn't just her stuff. It was theirs. They had worked on most of the house together. They had bought most of the things in that place together. Yes, their marriage had been short, but she had thought they'd put a lot into it in the time they had together.

Now, she didn't know what to do. And she hated that.

"You're thinking too hard again over there," Liam said, his voice low. She looked up at him, at that chiseled jaw and those piercing blue eyes. He had a hat on his head, but she knew he had a full head of dark brown hair that curled when it got a little too long.

Women flocked to Liam Montgomery, to the point where she wasn't sure if he would ever settle down. Not that she wanted him to, because she didn't know if she truly believed in the concept. Yes, some of her cousins and all of her siblings had found the loves of their lives. And Roxie had thought she had done that, as well. But she had failed at it. Tremendously.

So, she wasn't about to go and believe in anything that naturally happened again.

Not when she was purposely ignoring the ache in her heart—and her body at this point.

"I'm fine. Guess just a little tired since we went a little fast up that last hill."

Liam gave her a look that told her he didn't believe anything she had just said, but he didn't comment on it. Because that was Liam. He was just there for her. Just there. And that's what she needed right then.

She would put on her big-girl panties and face what she needed to, but not right then.

Now, she just needed time to breathe. And Liam would give that to her. When she did find those big-girl panties and pulled them on, then she'd face the rest of her family. And those pitying looks. Maybe even the judging ones. Because her family loved her, but they also wanted her to have the life that she couldn't have anymore. And she didn't quite know what to do with that.

"So, do you want to get some lunch before we head back to our respective homes?" Liam asked, twisting the cap back onto his water bottle before tossing it into the back of his vehicle.

They were each sitting in the backs of their SUVs with the hatches up, so they weren't truly sitting next to one another, but they were close enough. Others were starting to pack up and leave, waving and saying their goodbyes as they drove off. She and Liam were the last two left, and she had a feeling Liam was only staying because he was watching out for her.

So, he may not ask her any questions, and he may not crowd her, but he never really left her alone either. She had no idea if Liam had come down to ask her to cross-country ski because one of her family members had asked him to, or if he'd really just come down on his own. She honestly didn't want to know the answer, so she would never ask him. She was just sad he was there at all. Because despite the fact that she was the one who had asked for the divorce, she did not want to be alone, and the fact that Liam had to be there for her just meant that she'd made too many mistakes.

And while that might be a weakness, she didn't care. She had enough weaknesses, what was one more? One of the main ones: not being strong enough to actually ask the questions she needed to.

And...that was enough of that.

"I could eat. Actually, I probably should eat. I don't

know if I have anything in my house. I should probably go shopping."

Liam just shook his head, a sad smile on his face. "Okay. So, what we're going to do is go out to lunch, and then we're going to go get some staples from the grocery store."

He paused.

"Not the metal ones, like actual staples that you need in your house to eat. And then you're going to go home and do what you need to do, and you're also going to do this thing called online grocery shopping. It's this amazing new invention where you don't actually have to leave your house for food to come to you. It's one of my favorite things. Because I hate people. You know this. I hate people, I hate lines, and I hate carts coming out of nowhere and hitting me in the knees. They always hit me in the knees. Why is that?"

Roxie shook her head, a smile playing on her face. "You are a dork, Liam."

"Of course, I am. I'm a Montgomery. It's sort of what we do. But, anyway, you need food in your house, Roxie. You need to eat. You need to take care of yourself. And I'm not going to tell you why, because you know that. But you do need to take care of yourself. And if you're not going to do it, then someone needs to come in and do it for you, and I know that's not what you want. It may be what you need, but then again, we don't talk about that, do we?"

Roxie narrowed her eyes at him and threw back the rest of her cooling coffee. "Liam."

He held up his hands, a smile plastered on his face again. "All I'm saying is that we're going to go get some food, and then we're going to get some more food, and then we're going to order even more food. And maybe some cleaning supplies. I don't know, maybe something like a trash bag. I have no idea what you need in that house. But I bet you haven't taken a look in the past month. So, do what you need to do, and I'll be right there beside you, not saying a word."

She glared. "You sure are talking a lot right now for a man not saying a word."

"I can shut up when I need to. But I don't need to right now. And no one else is around us to overhear and have questions and want to ask you exactly what we're talking about. Because we're not actually talking about what we're talking about, so I guess that makes sense."

"Nothing you're saying makes sense." Of course, it did, but she wasn't actually going to let Liam know that.

"Well, if you're going to be nasty about it, I can actually say the name that you don't want me to say. Ask the questions that I'm pointedly not asking you."

This time, it was she who held up her hands in surrender. "Let's go eat. I can do with a steak. And eggs. Like really good breakfast food."

"That's my girl." Liam hopped off the back of his SUV and came forward to kiss her hard on the forehead. "I love you, Roxie. You're one of my favorite family members, even if I don't get to see you that often. And, yeah, the drive down here is a bitch, and I hate the fact that I have to wake up way too fucking early on the weekends to do it. But I'll do it every day that you need me to. Okay? Because I hate this for you. I hate all of this. You are so much stronger than you think you are, though. You just need to find that strength. So, we're going to go get you some steak and eggs because that sounds fucking fabulous right now. And then we're going to take care of the rest of the stuff that I can help you with. Because I love you, Roxie. Don't forget that. You are loved. You have always been loved. And you always will be loved. And I'm sorry you're going through this."

Roxie wiped the tears from her face, angry with herself for letting them fall. She had to stop crying. She was better at doing it in private but letting the tears fall in front of someone else just hurt. Because she didn't want Liam to know the depth of her pain. Didn't want anyone to know that she was broken inside. That she was an empty wasteland. She hated this.

Why couldn't she just be okay?

Why couldn't everything just be back to the way it was?

But, then again, what point did she want to go back to? The time before she had met Carter? When she had been alone but hadn't known what love—or loss—really was? She swallowed the bile surging up her throat and hugged her cousin before hopping off the back of her SUV just like he had. He closed the hatch for her, and she cleared her throat. He was always doing that, helping her even when she felt like she could do it herself.

Maybe that was the problem. Maybe she just thought that she needed to do everything herself. More than one person had told her that. And she had ignored them. Because it was easier to ignore them than think about what was wrong with her. Think about what was so unlovable about her.

She hiccupped a sob and started her SUV. She didn't want anyone to see her like this. She didn't want to *be* like this. But she didn't know any other way. Not anymore.

They found a diner on the way to her place, and she was happy that they were able to find a booth considering how busy it was. She didn't see anyone she knew, and she was grateful for that. Her neighbors had been very cautious about not asking her why Carter's truck wasn't in the driveway anymore. But she had seen the looks. Thankfully, she worked long enough hours that she rarely saw anyone. But it was getting a little harder to hide the fact that her husband had walked out. No, that wasn't right. He left because she forced him out. He left, because she let him walk away.

"Are you sure you don't want a side of pancakes? Because I think sugar heals all." Liam sipped his coffee, his eyes bright over the mug.

She shook her head. "I'm going to have steak and eggs and hash browns and everything greasy that's bad for you, but I'm not going to add extra sugar on top of that. Because I can have fats, but sugars are so not good for my hips."

He snorted. "I don't think you've ever had a problem with your weight, Roxie. Don't start now. Between all the cross-country skiing and your stress with your job, I'm pretty sure you've already lost too much weight. So, you're going to eat that whole fucking steak."

She winced and looked around to make sure no one had heard him curse. "Watch your language, Montgomery."

"You're the one who's making me curse, Montgomery-Marshall."

She froze. Wondering why he had said that name. She had hyphenated her surname because she loved being a Montgomery, but she'd wanted to show that she loved Carter, as well. Neither of them had said her actual last name in the past month. They hadn't mentioned Carter's name, and they had done their best not to talk about any of it. But, apparently, a month was just too much for Liam, and he was done tiptoeing around the subject. He wasn't going full-force, but he was laying down enough truth at this point that it was getting harder to ignore.

And Roxie really did not like it.

She raised her chin. "I'm not losing too much weight. I'm doing just fine. I'm just not going to add excess sugar to my diet if I don't need to." The words were clipped, and she knew it.

Of course, she knew her clothes were a little too baggy right then, but she couldn't help it. Between tax season and Carter, it was hard for her to actually think about shoving food down her throat so she could remain healthy. She was eating, getting exactly what she needed, or at least that's what she had thought. Yet, it wasn't enough, so Liam was calling her out on it.

"Just eat your fucking steak." She winced again and

almost tossed her creamer at him. But then the waitress came and put their plates in front of them. She had the steak and eggs with an extra side of toast because she loved dipping her toast in her eggs. Liam got the same thing, with a side of pancakes, as well as strawberry topping with whipped cream.

Her mouth watered just looking at it, and she almost ordered a side herself, but she knew she wasn't even going to finish her lunch, let alone an extra side of pancakes.

The two of them didn't talk about anything that was important, just about skiing and the antics of Liam's siblings. He had three siblings just like she did, but unlike her, he was the oldest.

She didn't know her cousins as well as she would like, but they all tried to stay in touch with social media. It didn't matter that all of them lived in the same state, they were all adults and had jobs, so it was hard for them to get together in person. It was only when there were big family groupings and gatherings that they got to meet up. Those were few and far between these days.

As soon as they finished, Liam paid, and she growled at him. But when they actually did get to go out to eat after one of their trips into the mountains, he always paid for her. She didn't know if it was pity or if it was just the fact that he was a male and that's what he liked to do. But she'd likely always argue with him because she enjoyed doing it.

He had to leave, so she went grocery shopping on her own because she was an adult and she could do this. Just because she had been ignoring what was important didn't mean that she would always do that. She was just having a bad time of it. But she *could* do this. After she'd picked up her staples, she went home, put everything away, and ordered even more groceries to get her by for a little bit longer. She just didn't want to deal with humans, didn't want to deal with the public. So, she didn't. And then, knowing she was sweaty and gross and probably shouldn't have been out in public like she was, she got into her shower and let the tears fall. Because she hurt. She hurt so damn much.

This time, it wasn't the pain in her legs or her side or her lungs. This time, it was the hollow emptiness that seemed to grow into a cavern in her body. She didn't want to die, but she didn't want to live like this anymore. She just didn't know the alternative.

She didn't know anything.

So, she let the tears fall, let them rack her body as she fell to the floor of the shower, crying until the spray grew cold and she had to wash out the conditioner in her hair using ice-cold water. But it woke her up enough that she could finish her shower and know that she would be okay. Because there wasn't another option.

And when she stood naked in front of her mirror, she wiped the rest of the tears from her face and put on her face cream and the rest of the things that helped her shield from the rest of the world, and knew that she would find a way to be okay. Because she had to be. She had to be brave.

Even if there wasn't a brave bone in her body.

She missed him.

She missed Carter so much.

And she couldn't help but wonder why she'd let him walk away.

CHAPTER SEVEN

Carter cursed as he scraped his knuckles against the engine he was working on before he pulled away, resisting the urge to put his mouth on the newly bleeding wound. He didn't need grease, dirt, and bacteria on it, and he sure as hell didn't need any of that in his mouth.

He wasn't supposed to be working on engines that day. Instead, he should have been in his office working on the mounds of paperwork that he still had to get through. He was so far behind on everything that he needed to do it was getting ridiculous, but one of his men had called in sick, and that meant he had to work on this engine. And then he had to work on an oil change, then maybe a couple of additional cars, and *then* he could take his work home—at least to the home that he was living at for the moment. And he would sleep with his paperwork surrounding him, the sad state of exactly what he was doing with his life like oil on the skin.

It had been a month since he walked out of the only home that had truly been a place that he could call that. He hadn't seen Roxie since, their schedules making it so he could get anything he needed from the house without having to bother her with his presence. She hadn't asked him where he was staying, but he had a feeling she knew, especially since he'd told her where he planned to start out, just not where he'd ended up. They were friends with the same people, but they were all doing their best not to talk about exactly what was going on. He hadn't seen any of the other Montgomerys since he left. Hadn't heard their words, didn't know if they hated him for what he had done. He owed them the courtesy of speaking to them and letting them know that as long as Roxie was okay, nothing else mattered. But he didn't know how to go about that. He knew that he likely wouldn't be getting another tattoo from a Montgomery, wouldn't be finishing the piece on his back he'd been working on for over a year.

He knew he wouldn't be walking into the bakery again, wouldn't be getting a cup of coffee and one of the cinnamon rolls that he loved. He probably wouldn't even be going into the tea shop owned by one of their friends. He wouldn't be picking out a blend that he knew Roxie liked whenever she was stressed out and needed to calm down.

He wouldn't be doing any of that. His friends were still friends of her family, but other than the men at his shop, he really didn't have any connections that weren't also hers. But that shouldn't have mattered because he *should* have been able to make it work with her. He should have been able to make it work so he didn't feel like he was doing everything wrong.

But ever since that night, ever since the loss that had changed everything, he hadn't been able to say the right words. And then he hadn't been able to find any words to say at all.

"Boss, you need help with that?"

He looked over at Anthony, one of his newer hires, and shook his head. "I'm doing fine, I'm just going to wash my hands and take care of this cut in the back. Can you take a look at this if you have a second? That way, I can make sure I don't screw anything else up."

Anthony nodded and hopped over. He was young, energetic, and made Carter feel ancient. Not that Carter was old, far from it. But these days, between the limp that he had whenever he got too tired, to his sleepless nights, and the fact that he felt like hell most days, he could have sworn he was in his eighties not his thirties.

"You're not screwing anything up, boss. I don't know why you think that." Anthony started humming to himself, his head down as he went back to work.

Of all of his men, Anthony was the only one who hadn't met Roxie. So, he didn't know what was going on in Carter's life. Of course, none of the other men truly knew either, but they had all heard that Carter was no longer sleeping at home. Carter didn't think that anyone knew there were actually divorce papers in play, but they did know that he was currently sleeping in Landon's guest room.

Carter had tried to move out a couple of weeks before, but Landon wouldn't have it. The man was a broker and used to be a financial planner, and it seemed he was going back to the latter soon. He refused to let Carter leave the house without a plan.

And considering that Carter didn't *have* a plan, other than to try and not fuck up his life any more, and not hurt Roxie in the process, he had just let Landon take over.

That probably meant that he needed to grow some balls, but he didn't really know what else to do. So, he stayed in Landon's guest room and tried not to take up too much space, just going about his day-to-day business. He needed to save some money, needed to just figure out what the fuck to do.

He just wasn't good at it, damn it.

And...he really needed those balls.

Carter went to the bathroom of his office and washed his hands before putting some ointment on his knuckles and bandaging them up. He had gotten an infection the first year he'd been working as a mechanic, and now he was doubly careful not to mess with his skin. Plus, his body might have healed from the fire, but he knew that one misstep could fuck everything up. He didn't have to fight the infection on his wounds anymore because those had all healed, but he still got achy in the mornings, and when it got really cold, he could feel it in every single bone and in every little tug on his skin. Thankfully, his wounds hadn't been as bad as he had thought at first. And for that, he was grateful. Because if it had been any worse, he didn't know what he would have done. He didn't know if he would have been able to stay at Roxie's—hell, at their place—any longer than he had. Yeah, he would have needed to if his healing required it, but thankfully, he hadn't. And he sure as hell didn't know what he would've done if he'd had to stay away from the shop any longer than he had been forced to.

Because he was working himself to the bone, trying

not to lose the only thing he had left. He had put every-thing he had into this place before he found Roxie. He'd done the same thing when he tried to put all of himself into their lives, only it hadn't worked out. His shop was in the black, but just barely. If he missed any more days or got any more behind, they'd be in the red, and that loan paperwork would start to curse at him and haunt his sleep.

Carter really didn't want to deal with that, didn't want to lose everything he had left.

So, he'd fight for this, even though he had tried to fight for everything else and failed.

And that was enough of that. This whole poor-me situation was really getting to him, and he just needed to work and not think about anything else.

Of course, as soon as he thought that, he walked out and saw Landon and Ryan with their coats on, looking completely opposite of one another.

Landon had one of those knee-length, black coats on that looked double-breasted like a peacoat and was very fancy. He looked like he should be walking down the streets of New York rather than into a mechanic shop in Colorado Springs. Ryan had on an old, beat-up leather jacket with the collar of his flannel showing. They both had tattoos, but Ryan's were far more visible. Landon did his best to hide his from the rest of the world since not everybody trusted their money with a man who had tattoos. Carter had a feeling that, eventually, his friend would say fuck it all and get a hand tattoo or something as equally in your face just to mess with people. Because that was Landon, he would screw with people if they tried to judge him.

"What are you guys doing here?" Carter asked, walking up to them. He held out his hand and gave each of them one of those half-hugs that he didn't really understand.

"We're taking you to lunch."

Carter raised a brow. "Seriously? You never come here to take me to lunch."

"That's not quite true," Ryan said, shaking his head. "We've tried, but you were always in your office on the phone dealing with some distributor or another or were too busy. But this time, we're not taking no for an answer. We will kidnap you if needed."

"And while I may look slender and very suave, I can still kick your ass." Landon winked.

Ryan snorted, rolling his eyes. "Really? Who the hell calls themselves suave?"

Carter couldn't help but smile, the first real one to cross his face in what felt like far too long. "You're both idiots."

"So? Though if we're honest, don't you think that

one of us is far more of an idiot than the other?" Landon said it with such a sophisticated tone, one that almost bordered on sneering, that Carter nearly punched his friend and roommate in the face.

Landon had done so much for Carter, and so had Ryan. The two of them hadn't let him feel totally isolated and alone. But there was still a part of him that did. That was.

"I've got a lot of work to do today, guys."

"So do we. And we don't give a shit. You're coming to eat lunch with us. We won't even take an hour. But you're going to have some food. And you're going to actually have a conversation. And you're going to try to not cover yourself in grease."

"You guys..." But he didn't say anything else. Instead, he shook his head and walked away, knowing he was beaten.

Because, frankly, he missed doing those things. Landon worked long hours like Carter. Plus, the man was dealing with his own relationship issues with Kaylee, not that Carter actually knew anything about it because Landon was worse than Carter at explaining himself and talking things through. Well, maybe not worse, but similar enough that it was eerie.

"Hey, guys, I'm going out to lunch. Handle the fort?"

Anthony and the others nodded, waving Carter off.

"Take your time, boss, it's good to see you getting out and about." The others glared at the younger guy as if they'd been talking about Carter behind his back. Hell, they probably had been. Anthony just shrugged it off and went back to the engine.

Carter shook his head, wondering what the hell he was going to do with these guys and the fact that they cared about him. He didn't know how to repay the fact that they hadn't let him feel alone. Just like Landon and Ryan were doing now.

The three of them walked to a local café that wouldn't mind the fact that one of them was in a suit, the other in jeans with a flannel over a Henley, or that Carter was covered in grease. He'd tried to wash most of it off, but he knew it was futile most days.

He ordered a Reuben with a side salad since even though he really wanted some fries, he didn't work out as much as he used to, and didn't go on his walks or hikes with Roxie. Those were the times where he had worked out the most. That and being in bed with her... not that he was going to think about that. Nope, wouldn't think about that at all.

"So, you want to talk about it?" Landon asked, playing with the ice in his Diet Coke.

"There's nothing to talk about. You know that. I'm in your guest room."

Ryan leaned forward, concern on his face. "You know Dimitri, Mace, and Shep would be here. I told them I was coming. But it's going to get awkward. More than it already is. You know?"

Carter stiffened for a moment before giving his friends a tight nod. "I know. It's not even them taking sides because there are no sides in this. There's Roxie and her family, and then there's me. A non-Montgomery. Never was, never will be. I get that. And you guys don't have to take sides if you don't want to either. Because Kaylee and Abby are both Roxie's friends. So, if it gets awkward for the two of you, know I'm not going to judge you for that. Okay? I understand if you need to stand by your women."

Landon held up a finger. "First, Kaylee is not my woman."

"Bullshit," Ryan coughed into his hand. Carter snorted but let Landon continue.

"And second, we are your friends. The others are your friends too, but they are literally married into the family or are blood. And I think once you actually sit down and talk to your wife, maybe we won't have to take sides at all."

Carter sighed. "Landon."

"No, you need to talk to your fucking wife. I don't know exactly what happened, but I do know that you were sullen and not thinking about anything but making sure she was okay. Because that's the kind of guy you are. You're the knight who does whatever it takes to protect his fair maiden. But your fair maiden needs a conversation. And so does the knight. Both of you deserve that. I just don't understand it."

"Landon," Ryan said, his voice low. "We're not here for that. You know it."

Carter shook his head again. "There are things you don't know."

"Things you won't tell us. But I get it, it's hard. Believe me, I know. But if you're just going to give up, then give up completely and move on. Or do something. Because it's killing me to watch you like this. And it's killing me to watch Roxie the way she is. Even though we don't see much of her."

Carter's head shot up. "What?"

Ryan was the one who answered. "She's basically cut herself off from the family, dude. She doesn't come into the shop, doesn't come in for tea or coffee. She's missed a couple of game nights and family dinners. She says it's because of tax season, but Shea still comes."

Shea was Shep's wife and also an accountant. She

had a little girl, as well. Carter barely resisted the urge to wince at that thought. A little girl. Dammit.

"So, you don't know if she's okay then?"

"Maybe if you asked her, you would know?" Landon snapped and then ran out of breath. "Sorry. I'm stressed about other things, and I'm taking it out on you."

"Don't worry about it. I probably deserve it."

Ryan just looked between the two of them before looking like he was about to give up. "Roxie's so far into her head it's a little unnerving. Just like you. But I know the two of you will figure it out. Because you have to. I know you have to. Now, what I know about Roxie? She's breathing a bit. Taking space for herself, I think. She's off doing that cross-country thing with Liam."

Carter didn't know why, but his gut clenched. Who the fuck was Liam? And why did the fact that her going cross-country skiing—something she hadn't wanted to do with him because she'd said she didn't want to do it anymore or was too busy and would rather just spend time with him—hurt so much?

"Liam Montgomery," Landon added, his voice low. "As in her cousin from Boulder."

Carter did his best not to look like he was being in any way soothed by that sentence. Because if he were, then that would mean that it mattered whether or not she might be moving on. It shouldn't matter. Because they were not living together anymore. They weren't talking anymore.

They were going to get a divorce.

They were not Roxie and Carter anymore. If she wanted to go out with a man named Liam, then she should be able to. But the fact that Liam was her cousin helped just a little. Carter was going to be at least a little bit honest with himself, even if he didn't actually say it aloud.

"I hate this." He hadn't meant to say that, but he was kind of glad that he did.

"We hate it for you, too." Ryan's words were soft, and the three of them paused in their conversation for a moment as they got their food.

"What are you going to do, Carter?" Landon asked, playing with his chips.

"I love her. I love her with everything that I am. But after things change, when you lose things, when you realize that you're not enough, you discover that love is not enough. And I'm not going to fight for something that doesn't exist. I'm not going to degrade what we had, or at least what I *thought* we had because I thought we could be something more. Roxie doesn't love me. She might have loved me before, but she doesn't now. I don't see it in her eyes. I didn't hear it in her words. So, yeah, I'm walking away because she wants me to. And I hate myself for it, but I can't change it."

His two friends just looked at him, confusion on their faces. Yeah, he could relate. He was confused, too. But it had been a month since he last talked with his wife. A month since he had walked away.

And he just didn't know what to do anymore.

Because they had lost something. They had lost something vital between them, and then that loss had turned what they had into something deeper, darker, and more depraved.

There was no coming back from that.

There was no working through two people who just didn't know each other anymore.

And Carter guessed this was really the end. Because it had to be.

CHAPTER EIGHT

Roxie had found her big-girl panties. They were hiding behind her period grannies and the fancy ones she wore daily. But now that she'd found them, she wasn't sure she was actually ready to wear them.

But knowing they were there meant she could do something brave...like invite her sisters over for dinner and wine, something she hadn't done in months.

It had been far too long since Thea and Adrienne had been to Roxie's house for dinner. In fact, she couldn't actually remember the last time it had happened. Thea had them over more often for game nights and meals. Adrienne usually let Thea or their parents do the inviting because Adrienne's house wasn't as big, and she was in the process of moving into

Mace's. That way, Mace's daughter, Daisy, wouldn't have to move again in such a short timeframe.

And Shep and Shea had just come back to Colorado Springs. Well, not really *just*, considering the tattoo shop was already up and running and doing amazing. It felt like everything was moving far too fast, and Roxie was struggling to keep up.

So, she knew that she needed to be a part of her family once more. Because the problem was, she had tried so hard to make herself who she needed to be so she could feel whole again that she had pushed everyone away in the process.

Including Carter.

She knew that now... Knew that she hadn't spoken to him. She hadn't told him what she was feeling, hadn't really told him anything when everything had first happened. Instead, she had gone into herself, trying to pretend that everything was okay. And when it wasn't okay, she had messed things up.

Now, she really didn't know what the next step to anything was, but she knew she had to stop being so insular. And in order to do that, she needed to be a Montgomery again. She needed to see her sisters. She needed to stop ignoring their calls and texts, and she needed to stop thinking that they were just going to rush in and try to fix things for her. Because they hadn't done that yet—and hadn't done that at all if she truly thought about it.

Yes, they always worried about her and wanted to help. But they never took over. They were amazing like that, and Roxie had to remember that.

Before she could get too far into her thoughts and actually convince herself to cancel this whole thing because she was too worried about how she would react, there was a knock on the door, followed by a doorbell ring, and the sounds of laughter on the other side of the panel.

Her sisters were here.

Roxie didn't know why she was nervous and excited at the same time. Oh, yeah, it was because she had pushed them away while trying to push away from herself.

Of course, that's why she felt this way.

"Hey there," she said as she opened the door, trying to make herself look like she was doing just fine. She was anything but fine, but she wasn't going to think about that right then.

Wow, she sure said that to herself often these days.

Adrienne grinned at her, her long, dark hair piled on the top of her head. Thea just shook her head and rolled her eyes and smiled at her, her hair flowing in the wind, looking slightly different since she had added a set of honey highlights to it.

Her sisters looked very similar with their bright blue eyes and their intense features. Roxie had always looked a little bit different, her hair a little lighter, her eyes a little darker. She more resembled Shep, but he was over a decade older than she was, so it wasn't like they had actually looked like each other when they were kids. But Roxie had seen pictures, so she knew that her features appeared much like his. And Shep and Shea's daughter Livvy resembled Roxie when she was a little girl.

"What's with the eye roll?" Roxie asked, moving out of the way so her sisters could walk into the house.

"Because I expected this long speech or some awkward silence, and I had no idea what would happen, so I got really nervous and rolled my eyes like a dork. I'm sorry. I have cheese. Of course, I have cheese. I'm Thea Montgomery, I always have cheese."

She held out a beautiful charcuterie plate complete with at least five cheeses, a few cured types of meat, some honey, chutney, and a couple of other things to use with that cheese. Thea was probably the best baker Roxie knew. And yet, her sister also had this oddly orgasmic relationship with cheese. Considering that

Dimitri had a very similar relationship, Roxie was glad that the two had found each other.

However, their passion for cheese meant that Roxie would never go hungry when it came to the dairy product.

And now that she had said cheese on her mind, she realized she was starving.

Thankfully, they had a whole plate of it.

"Seriously?" Roxie just shook her head, taking the plate into the kitchen. "That's how you start this off?"

"We've never done this before. I'm not very good at this whole awkward thing. I mean, my whole life is awkward, but you already know that."

Roxie just snorted and poured the three of them glasses of wine. She didn't even have to ask them what kind they liked. As she handed over the glasses, Adrienne shrugged off her coat, and Roxie took it and Thea's to the coat closet.

The three of them settled in and did their best to pretend that everything was fine, even though it wasn't.

"I have no idea what I'm doing. And I'm sorry that I'm acting like a dork. And I'm sorry that I pushed you guys away. I love you guys, but I don't know what I'm doing."

"What's going on with Carter, Roxie?" Adrienne

asked, her voice soft. "We love you, and we've done our best to give you some space, but we're worried."

"I thought Liam would have given you all the updates by now," she said, not really knowing if she was leading them or actually asking the question.

Both sisters winced, and Roxie knew that she was on the right track. "We're sorry, Liam doesn't actually report to us or anything." Her sister winced again and then set her wine glass down. "That sounds horrible. It's just that Shep and Adrienne and I were thinking that maybe somebody who likes to do the same stuff that you used to do would be good for you. But he doesn't tell us what you guys talk about. He doesn't even tell us when you go out. We just occasionally ask if you happened to go out, and he grunts or texts back. So, I'm sorry, it's just...we were worried about you and didn't know what else to do."

"I'm really sorry, too. We love Liam, we're glad that he's getting out of the house, as well. God knows he needs to. It's just that we didn't know what else to do, and we love you so much, Roxie."

Roxie wiped away a tear, but no more came. For that, she was grateful. She wasn't in the mood to start sobbing right then. "I figured someone had called Liam to tell him that I probably needed somebody. And, up until recently, he never bugged me. But now, he's bugging me, and I think it means that a month of me sulking and acting like a baby is quite enough."

"You're not a baby. And you're not acting like a baby."

Roxie shook off Thea's words. "Not dealing with my emotions or anything around me and diving into other things so I don't actually have to think about what's important? That sounds like baby behavior." Every time Roxie said the word *baby* she winced inwardly, but thankfully, her sisters didn't notice. Thankfully, her sisters wouldn't be looking too hard at her features when she said that word.

"What happened with Carter?" Adrienne asked again.

"I don't want to go into all of it. I know I need to. And I will. I just need to actually think the words on my own right now, and I can't even do that. And I need to talk to him. I don't know what else to do. Because of some things that happened, and because I don't think that we are the people we need to be for each other, I filed for divorce."

Both of her sisters just sat there, their eyes wide as they blinked rapidly.

"You asked for a divorce?" Thea asked, her voice deceptively calm. "You're the one who asked?"

Roxie nodded. She swallowed hard, trying not to

remember the look on Carter's face when he had seen the papers. "We haven't signed anything yet, and I don't know what else will happen. But it's done. It's over. And I think it has to be. Because he's no longer living here. He left as soon as he was healed. You guys know he's staying with Landon. And he's not coming back. In order for our marriage to work, there needs to be something that brings you together. Something that keeps you together. And I don't think we have that anymore."

"You don't know that, Roxie. You just said yourself, you need to talk to him. So, talk to him."

"I want to, Adrienne. And we tried. It just didn't work. He doesn't love me anymore."

"You don't know that, Roxie," Thea put in.

"I do. And that's the problem. Because if he loved me, this would have worked."

"Do you love him?" Adrienne asked.

Roxie wanted to answer, wanted to figure out exactly what she should say. But it was hard to tell somebody exactly what was going on in her mind when she couldn't figure it out herself. She loved the idea of Carter so much. She loved *him* so much. But it wasn't enough. She didn't like the person she had become loving him. She didn't like that she didn't know how to be herself, that she didn't even know who she was when she was with him. And that was on her.

And if she were going to figure out what she needed to do to find herself again and discover what parts of herself were left after everything had fallen apart, she couldn't be with someone that didn't love her. She couldn't be with someone that she was afraid she didn't love anymore.

"Sometimes, love isn't enough."

She hadn't noticed that her sisters had frozen, their eyes wide, until she heard the discrete sound of someone clearing their throat behind her. She stiffened for a moment and then set her wine glass down before standing.

"I didn't hear you come in," she said, her voice almost emotionless.

Her husband shook his head. "I didn't mean to barge in on you guys. I had to come here and pick up a few things I forgot. I didn't see the cars in the driveway."

"Mine's in the garage." She usually left it on the driveway. There wasn't a lot of space to do laundry out there, but without his car, there had been space for her car and laundry. She could see that his thoughts had gone along the same track as hers, and she wanted to wipe away tears. But there were no tears. There couldn't be when she didn't want to break right then.

Because it was the little things like her being able to put her car in the garage because his wasn't there that told both of them that this was becoming more permanent than she wanted to think about.

"We took a car service," Adrienne blurted. "That way, we could have wine. That's why our cars aren't here. Sorry, Carter."

"It's good to see you, Carter." Thea rushed to say the words and then winced before she and Adrienne stood up and murmured something awkward before going out into the dining room. Roxie was glad that they wouldn't be there to witness this, but she also missed them. She didn't want to do this on her own, and she knew that if she called for them, they would be right there for her. She was never truly alone with her family always there to support her. But why did she feel that she needed support when she was talking with her own husband.

"Do you need help?" she asked, not knowing what else to say.

"I'm fine. I can just come back later."

"Don't go." She blurted the words, and he looked at her, stuffing his hands into his pockets. She wanted to think it was because he was trying to keep himself from touching her, but she didn't want to put too much stock in that hope.

She missed his touch so much. It had been so long. She missed him.

She missed her husband so damn much.

"I'm just going to go and get a couple of things, and then I'll leave you guys to yourselves." He paused. "You're looking good, Roxie."

"Thank you," she said, her voice small. "So are you."

And it was true. Carter was looking healthier, even though the dark circles under his eyes were getting just as bad as they had been when they were each working too many hours. Despite that, they were starting to look like they were okay, like they were before everything had changed. And Roxie didn't know what to make of that. Because were they doing better and becoming more self-assured now that they weren't together?

That thought hurt the worst of all. What if the reason they floundered was because they were pulling each other down into that abyss?

"I'll be quick. You can tell your sisters they can come back in. I won't stay long."

And then he went to the guest room, and she could hear him packing a few things. She just stood there, not calling her sisters back, not calling for him.

And then he walked past her again, pausing right beside her before leaning down and kissing her cheek.

He'd kissed her cheek.

She felt the touch of his lips on her skin, and she could remember everything they had, and why it hurt so much now that it was gone. Because it wasn't just the fact that they weren't talking, it was that they weren't talking about the one thing that was the most important. It was something she wasn't sure she could give him. The thing that she wasn't sure she wanted. And it was the reason they were together in the first place.

At least in the abstract.

She was just so confused.

"I'll talk to you soon," Carter said quickly. "Because we need to talk, Roxie. Okay?"

She swallowed hard. "Of course. We do need to talk."

"Good."

And then he left. Suddenly, Roxie's sisters were back in the room, holding her close as she leaned into them.

But she didn't cry. Because if she cried, she'd have to acknowledge that everything was over and that everything was horrible. Because even though she knew that was the case, she could not admit it right then. All she wanted to do was eat some cheese, drink some wine, and pretend that everything was like it was before.

Only, it wasn't. Because nothing was like it had been. Nothing would ever be the same. Nothing had been the same since she had nearly bled out on the carpet and thought her life was over.

But now she was left just standing there. Her heart bleeding this time instead of her body.

And it was over.

It was really over.

CHAPTER NINE

Of all the stuff Carter could be doing today, the one thing he knew he needed to do was the single thing he wanted to do least of all.

Today had been a long time coming, and he knew that he just needed to get it over with, even if he would have rather been anywhere else right then.

He sat across from his wife, looking at anything but her because if he looked at her, he knew it would hurt too much. Of course, as soon as he'd seen her that morning when she first walked in, he hadn't been able to keep his eyes off her, even though it hurt almost more than he could bear.

They were sitting in a café that he didn't think they'd ever been to before, at least not together, and for that, he was grateful. He hadn't wanted to go some-place where they had memories. And he sure as hell didn't want to do it in the house where they'd shared so much, the building where she still lived, and the home he wouldn't be a part of anymore. He didn't think that any of her family members or even any of his staff came into this place, and that meant they'd be less likely to see anyone they knew. That was good.

He didn't want to deal with questions. Didn't want to deal with the stares. Didn't want to deal with much, other than what he was about to do. It would hurt. It would hurt something fierce, and he knew it was going to be like cutting off a chunk of his heart. He was going to do it. Because that's what he had to do.

He knew that love wasn't enough anymore, it hadn't been for a long time. So, he had called Roxie and asked her to meet him here. Asked her to come with the papers that he hadn't looked at since he'd glanced over at them when he first walked into the house from the hospital, in pain in more ways than one.

He would figure it all out. He'd figure out exactly what he needed to do to keep breathing. This is what *she* needed. She deserved a life where she wasn't constantly folding in on herself. Maybe he deserved something like that too, but he wasn't sure anymore.

He just knew that it wasn't working, and he wasn't

going to force something that caused both of them to hurt. Standing in a perpetual state of unease, pain, and failure only made the quicksand beneath your feet pull you down deeper, faster, and harder.

"Thanks for meeting me here," Carter said, his voice low. He finally looked at her and forced himself not to suck in a breath, not to reach out and brush the hair from her face. He forced himself not to beg her. Made himself not tell her that everything going on now was all a mistake, that they could fix this.

It wasn't what she wanted. It wasn't what they needed. At least that's what Carter told himself. He wasn't going to stand there and beg. Wasn't going to go to his knees.

Even though he wanted to.

At least, some part of him did.

"I didn't really know this place was here," Roxie said, tearing her gaze from him before looking around.

He missed those blue eyes of hers, he missed them more than he cared to admit. He might not see them anymore.

He knew that getting a divorce wasn't as simple as just signing papers, and he was going to see her again, but they would have to deal with everything that came. He was going to read over those papers and sign them.

Hell, he had read enough business papers when he

was opening up the shop that he could probably figure out what he should do.

But he would likely end up cutting out part of his heart in more ways than one when it came to what he was about to sign.

It was over.

He had to face that. Had to face it, even though it hurt him more than he wanted to admit. He cleared his throat. "I've driven by this place a few times. Thought it'd be better to talk here rather than at the house."

She turned back to him then, her eyes widening slightly. He wondered if it was because he'd called it the house and not their home. It wasn't going to be his home anymore. Couldn't be. He was going to make sure she got it. At least, that's what he planned.

He really didn't want to do this.

There were a lot of things he didn't want to do in life, yet he did them anyway. Things like taxes, grocery shopping, folding his clothes. This would be just like that, he thought. Except not in any way at all.

"I'm glad we're talking here. I brought the papers, but you shouldn't sign them yet." Her voice sounded strained, and he knew his probably came across the same. They had no idea what they were doing, but that was par for the course when it came to them.

"Why shouldn't I?"

"Because we need to talk about them. Go over them with your lawyer, and mine."

That made Carter's stomach clench, but he knew it didn't show on his face. Nothing did anymore. "Why do we need to go through lawyers? It's not like I'm going to fight you, Roxie. Anything you want, you get. Including the divorce."

She looked as if he'd slapped her—not that he'd ever raised a hand to her. He guessed he had sounded a bit gruff, but he had no idea what the fuck he was doing. He was messing things up left and right, and he needed to figure out what to do. He sure as hell knew one thing. This was a mistake. One that he would have to live with because there was no going back from this. She wanted the divorce, and he was going to give it to her. He'd just hate himself in the morning.

But as long as he didn't hate her, he'd be okay.

"I'm not saying we actually need lawyers, but you need to read over the papers. You need to make sure that the preliminary things I filed are right. I don't want to take anything from you, Carter."

She'd already taken his heart, what more was there?

"I'm sure everything you have is fine. I'll read over it now, though. You just sip your coffee, and I'll be quick."

She shook her head. "No, just read through it. Go slow. *Please*?"

Was she saying please because she didn't want him to sign? Or because she wanted to make sure that everything was thorough, and all the i's were dotted, and the T's were crossed. He just didn't know anymore, and that's how he knew it had to be over. He didn't know his wife. He didn't know anything about her. Didn't know what she wanted, or what she needed. He wasn't enough, and he had to face that. If he had been enough, he would have been able to figure out how to get her talking again. He would have been able to figure out how to pull her out of her shell so he could determine exactly what was wrong.

He hadn't been able to, and that was on him. Maybe it was on *them*, but it was mostly on him.

Carter let out a breath, knowing Roxie was right. He couldn't just sign legal papers sitting in a café without actually going over them. He didn't know if he really needed a lawyer, but maybe he would talk to Landon. Landon wasn't an attorney, but his friend would likely know what to do. Carter was so far out of his depth, it wasn't even funny.

"I'll take them with me and go over them."

She nodded quickly, both hands around her mug of coffee. Her hands were always cold, Carter remembered. Even in the summer, sometimes, she would burrow into him while they slept. He'd be sweating under all the blankets she liked to use, but then her cold hands and feet would touch him, and it would be like he was out on the tundra again.

He remembered that they'd gone to the doctor to make sure she was okay, that with everything else that had happened it didn't have to do with her cold hands and feet. The blood circulation in her body had nothing to do with what had happened. At least, that's what the doctors had said. He didn't know what they might have said recently because she hadn't told him. He had asked, but she had blown him off. So, he hadn't asked again.

That's why this was both of their faults. And that's why it didn't work.

"This is your copy. I have mine, as well. When we go through it, we can come together again and talk about it, or through our lawyers. Then we can figure out the rest because...this is it." She paused. "Right?"

He froze, not expecting that question. Roxie had been the one to file, even though they had both started to walk away from each other long before this.

It wasn't supposed to hurt like this, he reminded himself. Then again, maybe it was.

"I'll look over the papers quickly and get back to you." He sat there then, just for a moment. What else could he say? Was there anything at all he *could* say? "I should be getting back. Can't leave the shop for too long."

Something flashed in her eyes, but she didn't say anything. They never did. So, Carter stood up, leaned down, and brushed his lips over her cheek. He didn't know why he did that. It had to be the stupidest thing he could do. But he was being an asshole. Being an idiot. This was the second time he had brushed his lips along her skin since he moved away. The second time, and he liked it way too much. Had both times. He didn't even remember what her lips felt like at this point, it had been so long since they kissed. It had been so long since they touched.

Even with all the pain, even while walking away, it had felt like a reflex to lean down and brush his lips across her cheek. He missed the feel of her skin beneath his. He missed so much about her.

Both times he'd done this, she'd stiffened, and she didn't look at him or speak. So, he turned, not apologizing, because in a way, maybe it was goodbye. Perhaps, he was walking away from what they didn't have anymore.

He lifted his chin in another way to say goodbye and then walked out of the café, leaving his coffee mug full and still warm. He didn't feel like drinking it, didn't feel like eating.

And he wasn't going back to work. He had taken the day off, even though he really shouldn't have. His guys could handle things. They had shown that they could run things when he was in bed, unable to move because everything hurt so badly.

But now, he was okay. He was healed.

No.

He was broken.

He was beyond broken.

He was just so damn angry. Why couldn't he have figured everything out?

Why was it so hard to ask the questions that hurt the most? He had tried, he had damn well tried, but he hadn't tried hard enough. Or, maybe, no matter how hard he tried, it just wouldn't work out.

He was going to walk away because that's what Roxie needed. Because he loved her that much.

And he hated himself for it.

He drove to Landon's, his hands gripping the steering wheel so hard his knuckles turned white. Bile rose up in his throat, and he was shaking so badly that he barely made it up to the guest bathroom before he emptied the contents of his stomach. It wasn't like he had much in there though, because he hadn't been able to force anything down that morning before he met with Roxie. His body hurt, his heart hurt. Everything just hurt.

He had no idea what to do next.

He was rooming with a friend, didn't even have a place of his own. His wife was alone in that big house, the one they were supposed to fill together. They hadn't.

They hadn't done anything but grow apart.

That's when Carter's eyes burned, and the tears finally fell.

His body shook as he tried to get ahold of himself.

His marriage was well and truly over.

He wasn't going to get a second chance.

He'd lost that when he lost Roxie. He had lost that long before the explosion, long before they had missed a few game nights because they hadn't been able to sit in the same room with each other and actually speak.

He had lost her, and that was it.

Now, he needed to grow the fuck up and figure out how to be the man that he couldn't be for her.

He threw up again, then brushed his teeth and wiped his face. He slipped off his shirt, ignoring the tug on his new skin. He was pretty well healed up, he just sometimes ached in the cold. Considering that he lived in Colorado, he would likely ache for a while yet. He looked down at his body, over the muscles he had built with hard labor and the sweat on his brow over time. He hurt. But there was nothing he could do about it now.

He was blue-collar through and through, even more than the Montgomerys. Roxie had gone to college, so had Thea and some of the others. They had all either gone to art school or something that was perfect for what they needed to do in life. Carter had gone to a vocational college right out of high school. He'd barely graduated from high school as it was, but that was because he'd had to work two jobs. Somehow, he had made it all work, but it hadn't been easy. He barely remembered sleeping during that time right after he lost his parents his senior year of high school. A head-on collision, and they'd been gone before he could blink.

Then, he'd been all alone. Though newly eighteen so the state didn't have to deal with him. He'd worked his ass off, bunking on couches much as he did now.

Hell, somehow, he was right back where he started, albeit twelve years or so later. Alone, without a family, without anything to call his own, and falling asleep on something someone else owned.

Fuck.

He let out a breath and then wrapped his hands using the tape that Landon had given him. Then, he walked down to Landon's basement where the man had set up a mini gym. It wasn't as suave and sophisticated as Carter would have pictured, but there was a treadmill, and a punching bag, as well as some weights in the corner. It wasn't much, but Carter didn't need much right then. He just needed to punch the shit out of something.

So, he did. Right and left, left and right. He jabbed, did an uppercut. He just kept going until he knew his knuckles were bleeding, and sweat poured down his body. He hadn't even known that Landon and Ryan were in the room until Ryan cleared his throat, and Landon put his hand on Carter's shoulder.

Carter was exhausted, but he didn't swing around and punch his friend in the face. He honestly didn't care enough to do anything just then.

"Let's get you drunk." Landon's words punched through the fog, and Carter looked up.

"What?"

"We're taking the day off, something I swear that Landon has never done in his life," Ryan began. "We're going to get drunk, and you're not going to think about anything until tomorrow."

"Maybe that's the problem. Maybe I'm just not thinking enough."

"Well, we're not going to start tonight," Landon said.

"First, we gotta fix your hands. Fuck, man, you need your hands for work. Why didn't you tape them up better?" Ryan asked, and Carter just shrugged, knowing he was an asshole, but he just didn't care about anything anymore. Maybe tomorrow he would care. Right then, he didn't give a flying shit.

"Let's just take care of you, buddy. Tomorrow... tomorrow we'll deal with the rest."

Carter tried not to think about the sadness in Landon's voice, or the pity in Ryan's. Or the fact that his other friends—Dimitri, Mace, and Shep—weren't there. They weren't going to be there. They weren't going to come. Because they were Roxie's.

And Carter wasn't anymore.

He wasn't a Montgomery. Had never been. One day soon, when he moved out completely, Landon and Ryan wouldn't be his either. He knew that, and it was something he would deal with.

He hadn't worked hard enough for his wife. That was on him. Now, he had nothing left to give, nothing left to hold. He couldn't ask for more.

He didn't deserve it.

CHAPTER TEN

Roxie slowly slid off her dress, letting it fall to the floor on top of her tights and shoes. She took off her bra and panties, her movements wooden, her joints aching as she took another step toward her tub.

The tub Carter had bought and helped install because he knew she loved baths.

The one they'd paid extra for so they could get one big enough to soak together.

But she pushed those thoughts from her head. Instead of dwelling where she shouldn't, she slid one leg into the tub and then the other before sinking to her shoulders in the scorching-hot water. Her skin pinked, practically burning in the too-hot liquid.

But she didn't care. Didn't really feel a thing.

How could she feel anything when she was numb?

The tears didn't fall, not yet.

But when she reached for the bottle of wine she'd set on the floor and took the first sip, she let the first tear fall.

Then the second.

Then a deluge of the rest.

Her body shuddered in the tub, water sloshing over the side onto her clothes as she finally let go. She finally... *Let. Go.*

And when she couldn't cry anymore, when the bottle was on the floor, still full because she couldn't swallow a drop beyond the first, she pulled the drain on her now-cold bathwater.

Then she stood up on shaky legs and pulled herself out of the tub.

She toweled herself off, letting the terrycloth fall to cover the puddle on the floor before she walked woodenly to her bedroom.

There, she stood naked in front of the mirror to her dresser, thinking about what she should do next.

She wondered who stared at her in the mirror.

Because it was not Roxie Montgomery.

And she was not okay.

Then she slowly, oh so slowly, slid her wedding

rings off her finger before putting them in the box on her dresser.

She ignored the white band on her skin, ignored the emptiness.

At least, for now.

Then she stared at herself once again in the mirror. Naked. Bare. Hollow.

Who was this Roxie Montgomery?

She needed to find out because she had to be okay.

She had to live to the next day.

She had to learn this new Roxie.

Because she had to be okay.

But she wasn't okay.

There was nothing *okay* about any of this.

Nothing at all.

CHAPTER ELEVEN

It had been a month since Carter signed the papers, though Roxie hadn't yet for some reason or another. It'd been a month since they started the proceedings to end their marriage, and Carter was definitely not ready for what his men were asking him to do today.

"No."

Tommy, one of the first men who'd started at Carter's garage when he opened the place, leaned closer as he wiped the oil from his hands. Carter had known Tommy from the first place he worked. The older man had taken Carter under his wing a bit before Carter had left the place to open his own shop, and then Tommy had come with him.

Carter had always appreciated the other man's

advice, and the two of them worked well together despite the reverse power dynamics.

Now, however, Carter didn't want to listen to a word the other man had to say.

But, apparently, he wasn't going to get his way.

"I really don't want to hear it," Carter said before Tommy could say another word.

"It's been a month."

"You think I don't know how long it's been? I know exactly how long it's been." It had only been a month since they signed the papers, but it had been far longer since he'd disconnected from Roxie. Damn, it even hurt to think her name. But it wasn't like he could change anything. Not now. Not when he had walked away, and she had done the same.

"All I'm saying is that Stacia is a nice girl, and you should take her out sometime. Nothing serious. Nothing with a promise. But something that can get you back on that bronco."

Carter glared at his friend. "Really? We're going with the word *bronco* here? I mean, we work on cars. Thought you would've said Mustang, or back on the track. Or whatever other metaphor you could come up with that means you think it's okay for me to go out with someone that I don't know when you sure as hell know I don't want to date again."

Just the idea of the word *date* made Carter's stomach roil. Hell, he hadn't been on a date since he'd met Roxie, and it wasn't like they'd really been on dates when they were married. They'd been too busy trying to make sure their life worked, and then too busy pretending that it did. There was no way he was going on a date with a woman he didn't know when he was nowhere near ready. But from the look on Tommy's face, the man he worked with wasn't going to stop pestering him about it anytime soon. Meaning, Carter would have to deal with this crap unless he said yes and just got it over with.

"I'm not doing it," Carter repeated. "Go get to work on that sedan over there. It needs its oil changed and a lube job, and the owner swore she heard something rattle, even though her husband said he didn't. Meaning, there's probably something rattling because it's her car and she's in it more."

Carter didn't like the husband that had come in, but it wasn't like he was really able to judge. The man seemed the kind to walk all over his wife and tell her exactly what was going on rather than letting her speak on her own. Didn't make much sense to Carter. But then again, he hadn't been able to make his own marriage work. How was he supposed to know what was going on with anyone else?

"I'll take a look at it, but only if you agree to go out with Stacia. Not tonight. Maybe not even this month. But, sometime. Just consider it."

Carter narrowed his eyes. "Really? You're not going to work like I'm ordering you to? Talk about insubordination."

"Boy, don't even start with me. I only want what's best for you."

"Then go work and let me do what I need to do."

"If you had done what you needed to do, you wouldn't be in this mess," Tommy mumbled under his breath, and Carter closed his eyes, holding back a groan.

None of his men talked back to him like that. They all respected him and listened to what he said. Carter was a damn good mechanic, and he knew what the fuck he was doing when it came to his job. But his life? He apparently had no idea what he was doing there and sucked at the whole marriage thing. And just doing the right *thing*.

But the fact that Tommy felt like it was okay to talk like that? Maybe Carter deserved it. Perhaps it was because, yes, they had a decent power dynamic between them and it was in their history, but Tommy had a lot more years on Carter, and was going on thirty years married to his wife, Shelly. Thirty years with the same woman, and he hadn't fucked it up like Carter had after only a little more than a year.

Maybe Tommy knew what he was talking about.

Perhaps it was time to actually get back on that bronco and try to figure out what to do.

Just the thought of that made his stomach twist again, clenching with the idea of being out on a date with another woman who wasn't Roxie. But that was the point. It was never going to be Roxie again. Thinking that he could be with her just didn't work anymore. They were in the middle of divorce proceedings, and he'd already signed the papers. She wasn't his anymore. And hoping that it would change, wishing that he could just get over it and everything would be okay wasn't going to work.

So, maybe if he went out with this woman, this Stacia, he'd be able to...not get over Roxie, but maybe think about a future where he didn't want to throw up at the idea that he was alone.

Maybe he just needed to get out of Landon's house and do something other than work, hit the gym in the basement, or drink beers while sitting in his room alone and reading a book.

His life existence pretty much sucked, the routine so barren of anything fulfilling that he was afraid he would end up a husk of the man he had once been.

But he needed to think on this a bit more. He needed to think it over, go through exactly what he could possibly do, and determine if he was making the right decision. He was always a thinker, ever the quiet one. His parents had always wondered why he took so long to make a decision, and that was because Carter went over every outcome he could possibly foresee, afraid that he would end up with one he couldn't see at all.

He hadn't seen the fact that his parents weren't going to be alive past his senior year in school. He hadn't seen the fact that he was going to end up alone and practically homeless multiple times in his life.

He hadn't seen it because he hadn't *let* himself see it.

So, maybe he needed to just jump into something and see what came of it. Because for all his planning, nothing ever worked the way he wanted it to. Nothing ever worked the way he needed it to.

So, Carter let out a breath and went to help Tommy with the sedan.

The other guys who'd gone out to lunch were working on the other side of the garage, so he and Tommy wouldn't be overheard during their conversation.

"I can handle this on my own, you know. Think I'm

getting too old and frail?" Tommy asked the question, but there was laughter in his voice.

Tommy was in his fifties, he wasn't anywhere near retirement age. Of course, being a blue-collar worker without a college degree sometimes meant that retirement came later for some people. Though, these days, that wasn't always the case. Landon lamented that he was going to be eighty by the time he could safely retire, even with his nest egg.

Times apparently sucked for everyone, not just for Carter. He had to remember that. It should have warmed him at night, knowing he wasn't alone in the fact that he truly did not like his life. But it didn't.

"I know you can handle it, old man. Just let me get some grease under my fingers."

Tommy huffed. "I think there's grease perpetually under our fingers. You know my wife had me go and get a manicure once?" Tommy snorted, and Carter smiled. Fucking smiled. It had been way too long since he had done that.

"Really?"

"Yeah. I went along because she's my wife and I love her. But the audacity of it all... The *inhumanity*."

"Did you go with the pale pink or a fuchsia? Or maybe a blue to match those eyes of yours."

Tommy flipped Carter off with his greasy middle

finger before going back to work. "I had no polish other than a clear coat. It protected my hands from a lot of the grease for at least two hours. Maybe we should have the men in on this."

This time, Carter laughed outright. "Oh, yes, I can put an end to the work regime. You get a good workout and get your nails done."

"Hey, don't knock it 'til you try it. I'll probably never do it again, but it was for our daughter's wedding, and I promised I would not look like I had just rolled out of my coveralls and out from under a car."

"That makes sense then." Carter paused, then cleared his throat. "So, did you go for the pedicure?"

"I will not answer that."

"So, you went for the pedicure."

"Let me tell you, my feet have never felt so smooth. Like a baby's bottom. I didn't need it, but my wife wanted someone to sit with since we had to drive out to my little girl's wedding. Shelly didn't get to do a lot of the mother/daughter things because we both worked so much. So, I made sure that she got to get her pedicure and manicure and I got one right with her. Let me tell you, my wife was never so happy as when she walked in looking pretty as a picture. My daughter was pretty happy too, seeing both of her parents looking like they hadn't worked a sixty-hour work week for once."

"I'm glad to hear it. How long has your daughter been married again?"

"Going on eight years now. A little ridiculous when you think about it. I think I could be your father at this point."

"Yeah, maybe if you started a bit early."

"No, you're right about my daughter's age. So, yeah, I could be your dad." He paused as they worked, and Carter knew Tommy was thinking about what he wanted to say next. Tommy was a thinker just like Carter. That was probably why the two of them got along so well. And possibly why, when they didn't, they butted heads and then got over it pretty quickly. Because they thought about all the outcomes and tried to work with the best one.

"I'm sorry for pushing you like I did. I just want you to be happy. And I know you haven't been happy for a while. But I don't know if that has to do with Roxie or just other things. But know, I'm here for you if you need me. Stacia works at the place next door to my wife. So, she knows Shelly quite well. She's pretty, single, has no kids. Apparently, she is really bright and smiles a lot. I don't know if the smiling will annoy you after a while, but I figure...why not try it out?"

"Maybe I will." Carter said the words, and bile coated his tongue, but he ignored it. He needed to take a step in some direction. Even if it was the wrong one. He knew Tommy wasn't going to back down, and he knew the other guys would likely have women for him, as well. And he knew Landon and Ryan would want him to be happy. All of his friends, meddlers and matchmakers.

And he was an asshole for resenting it.

"You tell me when, and I'll connect the two of you."

He and Tommy worked together some more, while the thoughts and reactions of everything that could happen ran through Carter's brain.

"Why don't you give me her number and I'll give her a call."

He said the words, and it hurt. It hurt so damn bad, but he ignored it. He was getting good at ignoring things.

"I'll be sure to let her know to expect your call then. That way, it doesn't come out of the blue."

"That'd probably be a good idea."

Then they went back to work again and didn't say anything more. Because what else was there to say? Carter was going to plan a date with another woman. Someone that wasn't Roxie.

He would just have to deal with that.

. . .

"So, have you ever been to this place before?" Stacia asked, her voice soft and sweet.

Carter tried not to be annoyed by that.

He was an asshole, but he was trying not to be.

"I haven't, but I heard good things about it from my friends. And you said you liked Italian, so pasta sounded like a good idea to me."

After he had left the shop with Stacia's number in hand, he had called her the next night, trying not to put it off for too long. And then he'd thrown up and wondered if that would be how he reacted to everything from now on. Probably wasn't good for his system, but nothing was these days.

As soon as she had agreed to the date and he cleaned himself up, he'd asked Landon where he should take a woman. Because the only places he could think of were locations that were filled with memories of Roxie. And he wasn't about to do that. There was no way he wanted to be in a place where he'd been with his wife—no, his *ex-wife*. There was no way he could do that to himself. So, he was going to start new. Start fresh.

Tomorrow, he would try to look for an apartment. Because it was time to grow up. It was time to move on.

It was time to figure out what the fuck he was going to do.

"I love pasta. Pasta probably loves me a little bit too much, but that's fine with me." Stacia grinned, showing straight, white teeth and a beautiful smile. She had on red lipstick and a red dress that flared out at the hips. The dress had sleeves that belled at the elbows, and it was good for winter since it was cold outside. Her long, dark hair fell in curls down her back and over her shoulders. She had bright brown eyes and pale skin. She was a looker, that was for sure. And Carter knew that, no matter what, this wasn't going to work out. She would be too sweet, and he would be too mean. And that was fine. This was just him getting back on the bronco, as Tommy had said.

He was going to kill the man for putting that saying in his mind.

"I'm a fan of pasta too, but then I have to work out extra if I eat it."

Stacia smiled. "Well, it looks like you work out plenty."

She blushed as she said it, and Carter tried not to fidget in his seat. What was he supposed to say on a date? He and Roxie had just clicked when they met and had gone out quickly after, enjoying themselves. They just worked. Until they hadn't.

He had no idea what to do with new people. He was really going to make a mess of this, and then he was going to have to explain himself to Tommy.

Or maybe Tommy would have to explain himself to Carter since Carter knew he was nowhere near ready for this.

But, somehow, he made small talk and didn't talk about his family. Didn't talk about anything important. And Stacia did much the same. He felt nothing for the woman in front of him. There was no spark, no chemistry. And he felt bad because he knew he was just wasting her time. Apparently, he'd made a mistake. He made a lot of them. He and Stacia were just finishing up dessert when he looked up and spotted another couple walking in. Two people that he instantly recognized.

He hadn't told Landon what day he'd be taking Stacia out and hadn't actually seen the man that day since their schedules were opposite.

But there Landon was, Kaylee on his arm, and the two of them glaring at each other before they both looked at him and glared some more.

At least Kaylee was glaring. Landon just looked resigned, but Carter knew it wasn't on purpose. Landon was here with Kaylee, the two of them apparently on a date even though they swore they weren't dating. Now, everyone would know that Carter was out with another woman.

Because Landon might have known, considering that Carter was here because Landon had suggested the restaurant. But now Kaylee knew. And Roxie would know.

Carter was making a mistake.

He'd made a mistake from the beginning. He shouldn't be here. He missed his wife.

He missed her so damn much, and the idea that he was out with another woman just made him want to throw up again.

You shouldn't be here. You shouldn't be here.

He should be home, trying to work things out. He should be fucking talking to his wife and taking the steps they needed to figure out what was wrong between them.

He shouldn't have run away.

He shouldn't have done all the things he did.

He damn well sure shouldn't be on a date with another woman. Someone who seemed nice but whom he had no idea about and couldn't even truly think about without feeling like he was cheating on his wife.

Didn't matter that the papers were signed. Didn't matter that it'd been months since Carter had sat down with her and talked. Didn't matter that it'd been a month since he'd seen her.

This was wrong.

Stacia seemed to notice that something had changed. She smiled sweetly as they each split the bill and quit talking to each other. They had driven separately, something that he had done because he knew she would be worried about safety. He didn't mind that, but now, he was grateful for it.

"I can see you're not ready for this," Stacia said. "Shelly told me that you were married, and I think you still love your wife, Carter. Maybe you should think about what you need to do with that. Because you're a nice man. And you deserve to be happy. It's just not going to be with me.

He sighed, stuffing his hands into the pockets of his suit pants. "I'm sorry for this. I'm really sorry. I shouldn't have done any of this."

"Oh, I know, and I don't really feel too bad about it because I had a good night with a nice man. And I know that if I say we should be friends, you're just going to smile sweetly and politely say 'of course' and never talk to me again. Because I'm the woman you went on a date with while you were thinking about your wife the entire time. And that's fine with me. I'm just glad it seems like you're finally thinking straight. Now, go get her, Carter. Stop running. Go get her."

He had no idea who this Stacia person was, and he had no idea why she had come into his life at this exact moment. But, apparently, she was exactly what he needed to get his head out of his ass and actually do something that he should have done before. So, he said goodbye, didn't lean down to touch her, didn't even hug her. In fact, he realized that he hadn't touched her the entire night. He had nodded at her, doing a little wave when he first saw her, meaning he hadn't even shaken her hand or given her a hug when they first met. He hadn't made contact at all. And that was because he could only think about one person. His wife. The woman he should have been with all along.

So, he got into his truck.

It was time to talk to Roxie.

It was time to figure out what the fuck they were going to do.

CHAPTER TWELVE

Roxie moaned in her sleep, her dream too good to keep her awake. It didn't matter that she'd fallen asleep for a *nap* at four in the afternoon, she didn't want to leave this dream.

She kept her eyes closed, knowing she was halfway into her dream and half awake. She was going to pretend it wasn't just a dream. Because as long as she pretended, she didn't have to think about the fact that she was dreaming about Carter.

Carter's smooth lips, and his even smoother moves. She'd always loved the fact that he held her close after they made love, that he gently ran his hands over her to make sure that everything was just right and ensure that everything they had was exactly what they needed.

But he was always touching her, especially when they first got together.

And just like in this dream, he would run his hands down her body, touching every single inch of her until she was panting with need, moaning his name until she came. But he would never let her come. Not right away. No, he would make her wait, make her beg. And she knew that he was in as much tortured pain as she was. Because his hard cock strained against the zipper of his jeans or was hard and wet at the tip if they were naked. Because that's how they were with each other. Him wanting her as much as she wanted him.

But he didn't come, and he didn't let her come. Now, in the dream, his hands roamed over her breasts, plucking her nipples. She sucked in a breath, arched her back in her real bed even as she did so in her dream. Her hands roamed over her breasts in the waking world, even as dream Carter did the same for her there. She ground herself against his knee, on his thigh, wanting all of him. Wanting him inside her. His lips trailed over her breasts and then moved down between them and over her stomach. He left one kiss on each hip and then moved his head between her thighs, stroking her clit and kissing her lower lips. He bit the inner silk of her leg and then plunged his tongue deep inside her. She knew she would come on his face as if she were on a hair trigger.

But he kept going, holding her hips down with one arm as he used the other hand to keep plucking at her nipple. Or, he used that hand to finger-fuck her as he kept eating her out.

He was so good with his tongue. That beard of his a perfect rasp against her skin. She'd get a little bit of beard burn, and he would be apologetic about it, but she wouldn't be able to hold herself back. Just the thought of it made her want to come again.

And that's how she found herself, awake, wanting, and her hand inside her panties. She had orgasmed again, thinking about Carter. She really shouldn't be thinking about Carter. It felt so wrong. It *was* wrong. They were no longer together, and using memories of him as a way to get off, even in her sleep, felt like something she shouldn't be doing. Maybe if things were different, perhaps if they had worked out, she'd be able to make herself come by thinking of him. But, she really shouldn't. Given the fact that she had done so every single day this week, that just told her she had Carter on the brain. And she was losing her damn mind.

She resisted the urge to lick her fingers clean, blushing because that was something Carter always did. She had never needed to do it herself and sometimes found herself slightly prudish with sex, at least before Carter.

Well, she'd thought she was prudish. She'd had sex with her other boyfriends and had enjoyed it, had initiated some of it, and had generally liked the act. Then she'd had sex with Carter and realized what she could have.

She and her sisters talked about sex all the time, but she had been a little more reluctant to do so when it came to Carter. At first, because it was so personal and private between them, and then later because they weren't actually doing it anymore.

She hadn't wanted her sisters to know that, even though she had a feeling they already did. Or they had at the time. Now, they knew that she was definitely not getting any because they knew that Carter was no longer living with her and that he had signed the divorce papers.

She hadn't signed them yet. She would. She would soon. But she hadn't wanted to right after he did. Maybe it was because she was afraid of being on her own. But she was already alone, so she really couldn't use that as an excuse. It was more like she didn't want it to be the reaction to his action. He had taken time, they had both taken time after she filed the papers to sign. He had gone over them with Landon, and an outside source that she didn't know, and then he had signed them. She didn't even need to speak to him again.

That hurt to think about.

But she knew that she needed to sign those papers. She needed to grow up and do what needed to be done. After all, she had been the one to file them in the first place. Something her sister-in-law, Shea, had pointed out to her the day before.

Roxie had been slightly depressed and acting like a bitch. She hadn't been able to help it, but she knew she should have. She was an adult, after all. She had been a little despondent, going over paperwork in a café. It had been paperwork that had nothing to do with actual private information, so she didn't feel too bad about doing it in public. It was more just stuff for her own house. And in doing so, she had needed some space, some time to herself. And then Shea had walked in, wanting coffee, and had come over to say hello.

Roxie loved her sister-in-law, truly. But for some reason, when Shea had asked her how she was doing, Roxie had snapped.

"I'm fine. I just wish people would stop asking that," she had said, her voice louder than she expected. Shea just narrowed her eyes and then set her coffee down.

"We love you," Shea had said. "We love you so much. And we're here for you. But you have to let us help you."

"I don't need help. Carter signed the papers. It's over." She hadn't meant to say that, but it was out there, and there was no taking it back.

Shea just leaned over and kissed the top of Roxie's head, her eyes filled with tears. "You're the one who filed them, Roxie. And I love you."

There hadn't been much to say after that, and Roxie knew that she needed to get over herself and realize that Shea was just trying to help. Because nobody knew how to help her, let alone herself.

But now it was a Saturday night, and Roxie was losing her mind. She was taking a nap and having sex with herself while thinking about her soon-to-be official ex-husband.

She didn't know why...no, that was a lie. She knew exactly why that hurt.

Because Carter was supposed to be her forever. And he wasn't.

She was wearing a sweater dress, but she had taken off her tights earlier that day. Apparently, she had subconsciously known she would want to get herself off in her sleep and needed the easy access.

But because it was still chilly outside, and even

though her heater was going, she was still cold. So, she put a lap blanket over herself and pressed the button to turn on the fireplace. That had been a new addition to the house that Carter had helped put in. He was so handy, something that she had taken for granted. Because she had no idea what to do when it came to home repair. She would have to find a handyman because she couldn't even fix the drawer in her kitchen. She had tried, had gone on YouTube, and had almost called her brother or soon-to-be brother-in-law to help.

But she hadn't been able to do it on her own, and that had annoyed her. When had she truly been on her own? Ever?

She'd gone from her house, the one she had lived in with her parents and family when she was growing up, to her dorm room, and then had moved in with room-mates in an apartment building. After that, she had bought this house. She had been alone for just a little while before she met who she had thought was the love of her life, and then Carter was there.

And now, she was alone again.

But as soon as she thought that, someone knocked on the door, scaring her. She sloshed her hot tea, cour-tesy of Abby's tea shop, over her fingers and cursed. Thankfully, it wasn't too hot since she had fallen asleep right after she finished steeping it.

She shook her hand and then wiped her fingers on her blanket. She didn't even have a napkin with her. Hell.

She quickly stood up, tossed the blanket over the back of the couch, and made her way to the front door. When she looked through the peephole, she swallowed hard, wondering why it had to be now. Why, when she could still smell herself on her fingers, would he be there?

But she opened the door, raised her chin, and prayed that she wouldn't break all over again.

"Hi," she said, her voice soft, this time with emotion. Thank God. She was so afraid that she had somehow lost the ability to feel. Apparently, all she needed to do to remember was see Carter again.

Why was he here?

Why was he here tonight of all nights?

And why did he look like he had been out?

He'd smoothed his hair back and trimmed his beard. He wore his bomber jacket over a nice crisp shirt and gray slacks. He wasn't wearing a tie.

He looked like he had been out on a date.

And she hadn't been.

She was very aware that she still had sleep marks on her face from the pillow she had slept on. She also hadn't brushed her hair after her nap and looked like she had been sleeping away her Saturday.

She was living the life…at least sarcastically.

It seemed that he was actually living.

And it hurt.

"Can I come in?"

She automatically took a step back, gesturing for him to come in. After all, it had been his house for almost as long as it had been hers.

"Did you forget something?" Why was that the first thing that came to mind?

"I guess you could say that. I guess I forgot a lot of things."

She frowned, staring at him. "I don't understand."

"Seems I didn't understand a lot of things."

"Okay. What's wrong, Carter?"

"Everything's wrong." He turned on her and ran his hands through his hair.

"Then why don't you start from the beginning. Is someone hurt?"

"Not in the way you're thinking, but fuck, I don't know how to start this. I don't know how to say what I need to say."

She rolled her shoulders back, afraid. "Then just say it." Maybe if they had actually spoken like this before, they wouldn't be standing here right now, feeling like they were strangers. But that was for another conversation.

Or, maybe, maybe it was for right now.

"I was on a date tonight."

She hadn't realized she had taken another step back, and then another and more until her back was pressed against the door. She was shaking. She had known this time would come. They were getting a divorce. They were no longer Carter and Roxie. This was supposed to make sense. He was supposed to go out and find someone else. He was supposed to go out and be happy. That was why she was letting him go. But the fact that he had actually done it, the fact that he was here right after it?

Oh, God, she couldn't breathe. Why couldn't she breathe?

She put her hand on her chest, trying to calm her heartbeat. She knew her eyes were wide, and she knew her face was pale. She could feel all of that happening, and he just stood there staring. He put one hand out as if he wanted to help, but she couldn't focus, couldn't breathe.

Why couldn't she breathe?

This is what they wanted. So why couldn't she breathe?

"Oh," she said, though she didn't actually say the

word out loud. She'd opened her mouth to speak, but nothing had come out. Nothing ever came out like it should.

Why couldn't she speak now? Why couldn't she tell him that she hurt? Why couldn't she tell him that this was all wrong?

She needed to tell him that she wanted to be with him. She needed to tell him that everything would be okay. She should have said this all way before this. She should have told him that she was hurting and that she was in pain, that she had no idea who she was anymore.

She needed to say all of that *before* she gave him the papers. She should have said all of that before he left.

Now, he was here, maybe even smelling of another woman.

She had just been dreaming about having sex with him, about being with him, and he had been out with someone else.

She was going to throw up.

She was going to be sick.

She'd thought all the hurt was supposed to be over. She'd thought it was supposed to be gone.

But it was back. It was all back.

This is it.

She needed to say something.

And yet nothing would come out.

"I never touched her, didn't even hug her hello. It was a friend of a friend from work. Tommy's wife's friend. Not that you needed to know that."

"Oh." There, she'd actually said the word this time. What did he want her to say? What was there *to* say? "Why are you here, Carter?"

"Because I was on a fucking date, and all I could do was think of you. Why was I on a date, Roxie?"

She blinked. "I can't answer that for you."

"Well, I can't answer it either. Other than the fact that I just wanted to feel again, and now I feel like I'm making all the wrong choices and moves. I've been doing it for far too long. How did this happen, Roxie? How are we standing here, acting like we're strangers? You are my wife. Technically, you still are. And yet I can't say the words I need to. They're not even coming to mind when I'm looking at you. I shouldn't have left. I should've fought. I know it's too late now, yet I don't want it to be too late. I was on a date with someone else, and I shouldn't have been. She means nothing. And she knows it."

"I..." Roxie's voice trailed off. She was trying to catch up. He was here, saying all these things now? Why couldn't he have said them before? The papers were out. They had already walked away from each other. Why was he here again?

"I love you so much, Roxie. Or maybe I love what we had. And I know it's too late to go back to that, but I hope to God it's not too late to talk. Because we should've talked before. I know that everyone says that we should've talked all this time, but I couldn't. I couldn't face you and know what we lost, know what we might not ever have again. I couldn't do it. I couldn't do it because I loved you so much, and then I was afraid that I would hate myself and maybe even hate you in the end. Because I didn't know who we were anymore. But I want to try. I just want to try and figure out what happened. I should've done this before, but I couldn't. And that makes me a coward. A loser. I miss you, Roxie. Miss you so fucking much."

Tears ran down her face, and Roxie realized that this was the first time she'd actually cried in front of him in far too long. She hadn't wept when he got hurt. Not in front of him anyway. She hadn't cried when he left, not in front of him. She had sobbed endless tears over this man in private, had wailed over who she had become, yet this felt different.

She couldn't hate him for it. And she couldn't hate herself.

"I don't know what to say."

"And that's our problem. We never know what to say. And it's bullshit."

She blinked. "Excuse me?"

"It's bullshit for both of us. We were fucking married, Roxie. We still are. Why can't we just say what's on our minds and in our hearts? Why is it so hard?"

"I don't know why it's so hard. It was always hard. I don't know what to say anymore. I never did. And you walked away, Carter. You walked away without looking back."

"I walked away because you told me to go. Because you're the one who got the papers."

"You walked away a long time before that," she snapped.

"I was just following the path that you laid out for us."

A gasp. "That's a lie."

He shook his head, wiping his face with his hand. "Maybe it is. Maybe it's just what I thought. And maybe that's why we need to fucking talk. I'm not saying I need to move back in or that we need to go back to what we were. But we do need to talk. Because I miss you so fucking much. I don't know if you still love me, but I love you. I love you with everything that I am, Roxie. And I want to find out who we are now. I don't want to date other women. I don't want to be living in Landon's place. I don't want to go find a place of my own. I want to find the Carter that I need to be for the Roxie that you are now. And to do that, we need to talk. We need to...be."

She let out a breath. "Let this be, Roxie. Let us be. Just give it a try. That's all I ask of you. Just give me a chance."

"It was hard to talk before, and it's even harder now. You know what happened. You know what happened before."

"I do. And we never talked about that. That was our mistake. One of many."

"But what if we're afraid? What if we're even more afraid after we speak than we are now."

"Then we at least tried. I know we're in pain. I know we're making mistake after mistake. I know no one knows what to do with us. So, don't let me walk away again. Let's just try. That's all I ask."

"It's going to hurt more. To talk about the things we ignored. To talk about the why. To talk about *how* everything changed."

Carter came forward then and cupped her face. She closed her eyes, telling herself not to lean into his touch. She had missed this so much.

"So be it. If it hurts, then it needs to. I should've done this before. We wasted so much time."

"It might not work. We might realize that there was a reason we didn't talk, that there was a reason we're in this position."

"But at least then we'll know. Just don't make me leave again."

"I don't know what happens if you stay."

"No one does. But we need to figure it out. Together."

He didn't kiss her then, as much as she might have wanted him to, and she was glad. Because she didn't know what she would've done. Sex wasn't an option, not just then. They needed to actually figure out who they were together.

"What do you mean exactly? What are you thinking about?"

He let out a breath, his shoulders relaxing just a bit. But there was still so much strain on his face and in his jaw. "Let me take you out on a date. A first of sorts."

"A first date when we're technically still married?"

"It's what we need. At least, I think so. I miss you."

"I can go on a date."

She didn't say she missed him back. Maybe...maybe he already knew.

"Let's just figure it out."

"We'll do it together. Like we should have before."

And then he lowered his forehead to hers and just rested it there before letting out a shuddering breath and walking out of the house.

She had no idea what to do next, but then he texted her. He sent her a message telling her a time and place for next week.

It was Saturday, after all, and he knew that she would want to go to sleep early on a Sunday.

He knew that because he knew parts of her. She couldn't say that he knew all of her because she knew one of the reasons she was like she was now was because she didn't know who she was either. No amount of cross-country skiing and trying to figure out who she was on her own would help that.

She sent a text back, saying okay.

Okay.

She was okay.

Even if she wasn't okay.

She would go on a first date with her husband.

And she wept.

Again.

CHAPTER THIRTEEN

First dates were supposed to be awkward. Getting ready for first dates was supposed to be awkward. Getting ready for your first date with your almost ex-wife was as awkward as possible.

Carter rested his forehead on the wall next to his borrowed closet and wondered what the fuck he should wear to a date with a woman he loved but whom he was no longer in a relationship with.

He knew he wasn't going to wear what he had worn the week before on his date with Stacia. In fact, though he probably shouldn't have because it wasn't like he had money just hanging out on trees anywhere, he had thrown away everything he had worn that night, except for his bomber jacket.

That, he wasn't getting rid of. That he'd had the

night he first met Roxie. It was something he had worn for most of their nights out. Not just because it was special to him but also because it was special to him and Roxie as a couple. He also didn't have another jacket, so it wasn't like he could've worn something else when he went out with Stacia.

He didn't want to even think that woman's name again. She was very sweet and nice. And going out with her had jump-started his doing what he should've done all along.

Namely going over to his wife and begging her to talk to him. Begging her to give him another chance. And, maybe even begging himself to try and give *her* another chance.

If that made any sense at all.

Though, it wasn't like he made much sense these days. But he was trying. He was damn well trying.

Finally.

"Are you okay over there?" Landon asked, his voice very careful.

Carter opened his eyes and moved from the door of the closet so he could turn and face the other man. Landon leaned against the door jam, his arms folded over his chest. He looked like he had just gotten off work, even though it was Saturday, but Landon tended to work long hours and weekends these days. Sure, the other man was saving, they all were, but he was also hiding from the fact that he had feelings for Kaylee, and was therefore burying himself in work. Much like Carter had done.

"I have no idea what I'm supposed to wear."

Landon snorted, a smile playing on his face.

"You think that's funny? You think I like the fact that I'm nervous as fuck going out on a date with my actual wife? I shouldn't be this nervous, but I'm more so now than I was on the first date we actually had together. In fact, I think my palms are sweaty." He rubbed his hands on his pants. "Yep. Clammy as hell. What the fuck am I supposed to do?"

Landon held his own hands up, still smiling. "I'm only laughing because I had this exact conversation, well at least close to this exact conversation with Ryan on his first date with Abby."

Carter perked up. "Yeah?"

"Yeah. Ryan was nervous because it was his first date with her. Apparently, it wasn't Abby's first date since losing Max, but it was still an important date to her because Ryan meant something different. As we all know now. And Ryan was so nervous that he was going to fuck everything up, that he tried on like four different outfits until he finally found what he needed to. I was the one who actually picked it out for him, but we're not going to discuss that."

"Teach me your ways. Pick me out something."

"Are you just asking me that because I'm the only bisexual you know?"

"Fuck you." Carter flipped his friend off just in case his point didn't get across. "And you're not the only bisexual I know. You're not even the only bisexual in this room, dumb ass."

"Touché. But, I'm pretty sure every single one of us in our little group of friends is bisexual. It's starting to add up."

"No, it's a new world where you're actually able to talk about your sexuality and figure it out. We get it. You're allowed to be yourself. But, oh my God, I don't know if I can actually be myself tonight because I'm going out on a date with my wife. So, let's digress from sexual identity and politics and go into the fact that I'm going on a date with Roxie and I have no idea what the fuck I'm doing."

"You sure do ramble a lot when you're nervous."

"Once again, fuck you. But please, please for the love of God, help me figure out what to wear."

"Well, where are you taking her? Not the same place you took that other woman I hope."

"I'm getting really tired of saying fuck you, but just in case you missed it, fuck you."

"I'm just trying to help here. You keep telling me to fuck myself, I might just go and do it while you sit here standing in your jeans and your tank top, wondering what the hell to do. But sure, please continue telling me to go fuck myself."

"Landon."

"Okay, I know you're not going to the same place you took Stacia, and the only reason you did is because it was my idea. And, by the way, I didn't actually realize that you were going out that same night, or I wouldn't have gone there with Kaylee. Kaylee also said she wasn't going to talk to Roxie about it unless Roxie wanted to. Even though I know that Kaylee doesn't like to keep secrets."

"You don't have to worry about that, I didn't actually mention you and Kaylee to Roxie, but I can tonight if you want. But she knows that I went on a date with another woman. And she knows that it was a mistake. And now we're just trying to start over without actually starting over because it's the part that we keep not talking about and the other things in our relationship that got us in trouble to begin with."

"Okay. Good to know. And probably for Kaylee's *and*

Roxie's sake, you should probably mention to her that we were there."

"Well, when Roxie asks me why you were there with a woman that you're seemingly not dating, what should I say then?"

"Tell her we were there as friends."

"Bullshit."

"Only one awkward relationship at a time, Mr. Marshall. So, let's focus on you and Roxie, and then we can focus on whatever the fuck is going on between me and Kaylee. Not that there's anything going on between us. We're just going to ignore that I said that. And, you should wear black tonight, that lovely black shirt that you have that buttons all the way to the top, but don't actually button it all the way to the top. And then wear your dark gray slacks. With the black shoes that you slide into that don't actually have ties. Oh, and make sure you wear your watch and wipe as much grease from underneath your fingernails as possible. Not that I think Roxie has a problem with that, considering she married you knowing you're a mechanic and that's sort of your thing, but still."

"I've already washed my hands a few times." Carter held up his hands. "See? Pretty clean."

Landon looked him over, inspecting. "Good enough.

Just make sure that whatever goes on tonight, you're open. Because I know that you're completely closed-off most of the time. Hell, I don't even know as much about you as I probably should, given that you're living with me. Just not permanently, right?"

Carter let out a breath as he stripped out of his clothes and put on what Landon had told him to wear. "I'm not going to be living here permanently. If and when, or maybe just if Roxie and I decide that it's not going to work for real, I'm already thinking about what apartment building I'll move into. It needs to be near the shop but also near an area where I'm not constantly bumping into a Montgomery. That's harder than it seems because they're spread out all over the state."

"I know what you mean. But you're welcome to live here as long as you want, I wasn't actually pushing you out. Unless it's pushing you out into the arms of your wife, then I may be giving you a shove."

"You're all heart, Landon. Does Kaylee know how romantic you are?"

"Off-subject, Carter."

"Or rather, right on the subject, *your* subject."

"We're not discussing this. We *are* going to discuss what you're going to talk about with your wife, though."

"I have no idea. We can't go too deep into some things because we're going to be out in public."

"And where exactly are you going again?" Landon asked.

"A new place. One of those Asian places she loves. I think it's some Korean and Japanese fusion? At least that's what the menu said. It got high reviews, and I've driven by it a few times. The photos looked pretty mouthwatering."

"Good call. Don't go to the place you took Stacia, which now I'm afraid I may not be able to go to again."

"Sorry about that, though it was your idea to go there."

"Touché," Landon replied.

"But, really, a new place where you can start together. Don't go off down memory lane too far with the actual places while you're actually talking about it using words. Use your words, Carter. You have a great voice even though you do ramble sometimes. So maybe ramble and tell her exactly how you feel."

"I did a lot of that last week when I went over to the house. I'm going to do more. Because I have to. I love her, Landon. And I should've fought harder when it mattered."

"It matters now, too. Just don't fuck it up."

"There are no wiser words than that."

He let Landon inspect him once more to make sure he had everything in the right places. He had been dressing himself for years at this point, decades really, but if his friend wanted to make sure he was actually looking like a man going on a date with his wife, then he'd go for it. Plus, he was so nervous, he was afraid he would forget to zip up his fly or wear two different shoes or something.

He went to the house that he had lived in, the dwelling that he had slept under the roof of with the love of his life to pick up Roxie. Unlike with Stacia, Carter wasn't going to meet her at the restaurant. He had asked if he could pick her up, afraid that she would say no, but she had actually said yes.

Now they were going on what would probably be an awkward as fuck first date. But it was a first. It was trying. It had to count for something. Carter just hoped that it didn't count for everything and nothing all at the same time.

"Don't fuck it up," he whispered to himself before he knocked on the door.

She opened it, and he just about swallowed his tongue. She had on a cute black dress that wrapped around her middle. It flared out at the hips and went to her knees. She wore it over black tights with black knee boots. He had just seen a peek of the tights and knew they had an etched design on them, one that he wanted to inspect. But maybe not tonight. Perhaps tonight wouldn't be that. He shouldn't think about that at all. Not now, maybe not ever. Not if he actually wanted to have a real relationship with his wife.

Her hair was done up in long waves, but the top of it was pulled halfway back so it sort of bumped up in the back. He really didn't know what to call it, all he knew was that it framed her face in a way that made her eyes pop.

He fucking loved this woman.

And he hoped that with everything they put into this, that love could be enough.

"Wow," they said at the same time, and Carter smiled at her.

"You look beautiful," he said, his voice rough.

"I was going to say the same thing, but then I thought that beautiful wasn't the right word. I guess you beat me to it."

"I'm just happy you're coming with me. I made reservations for seven at Ko. We should have enough time to get there and maybe have a drink at the bar before we have to sit."

"That sounds wonderful. I've always wanted to go

there, but I just never made the time."

He paused as they made their way to his truck. "Then I'm glad we're making the time."

He knew he was talking about more than just their dinner tonight. He was talking about so much more.

He helped her into the truck because even though he had the step, she still had to hop up a bit. He put his hands on her hips and helped her in, both of them freezing for a moment, their eyes meeting.

He hadn't touched her like this in so long.

And yet, at the same time, he didn't know if he had the right.

One step at a time, he reminded himself. Just one step at a time.

They talked about nothing.

They were quiet in the car, their conversation stilted as if they didn't know what to talk about with each other. Honestly, he really didn't. The date was going well, but it had to go better soon.

They were able to get their table right away, so they soon found themselves sitting across from each other, each asking the other about their respective jobs yet not really talking about anything. It had been easier to talk to Stacia the week before, but that was because it hadn't been important.

Everything between him and Roxie was important.

So, when they sipped their drinks, waiting for their appetizer sushi, he let out a breath and leaned forward. He had to start somewhere.

"Do you remember the first time we met?" he asked, reaching out to rest his hand on hers. She didn't pull away.

Thank God.

She blinked and then met his gaze. "I do. A flat tire of all things." A small smile played on her lips.

Carter smiled at that, too. "You called in to the shop, my shop, and I didn't even know you had our number."

"I saw it as I was driving by one day, and one of my coworkers said you guys had done great work for her, so I kept the number in my phone just in case I needed it. As it turned out, I did need it."

"It must have been scary, having a blowout like that when you were on one of the side roads where the speed limit is pretty high."

"It was. But, somehow, I actually turned the wheel the way I was supposed to even though I didn't really know how I was supposed to and couldn't tell you right off the top of my head right now. But I made it, though the flat tire was more than I could handle."

"I know what you mean. People tend to make fun of others when they can't do something that *simple* as they call it. But when a tire blows like that, if you don't know if the hubcap or anything else is safe, then you need to ask someone for help."

"I'm not going to lie, I really didn't want to have to get down on my hands and knees in my suit and deal with it. Not to mention, I'm not the strongest person in the world. Getting those lug nuts off probably wouldn't have worked out too great for me. My dad and my brother tried to teach me how to do it once, and I listened—and I could probably do it if it was an emergency—but I honestly just needed help."

"And I drove up, and you were there."

They met gazes across the table, and he tried not to think about hope. He tried not to think about anything than just the present. Because they were talking more than they ever had. And that counted for something. Maybe if they could talk about the little things like this, they could talk about the big stuff, too. And, holy hell did they have big things. They just had to get there.

"Well, I was grateful that you helped me out. And you were pretty hot. I'm not going to lie."

He shook his head, moving back as the waiter took away their appetizer plate and put down their food. He had gotten the bulgogi platter, his favorite. She had gone with more sushi and a side of seaweed salad. He knew that if they were going with the way they used to be, she would ask for a little bit of his bulgogi, and he would eat a bite of that ginger and maybe a part of a roll. He just didn't know if that's what they were really going to do that day.

He'd always found it weird that he loved sushi and things that weren't just all-American. His family had been all brown butter and mac and cheese. Hamburgers and apple pie. As Southern all-American as you could get. And, sometimes, the twang in his voice came back, and he went to his roots, but it wasn't really who he was anymore. He liked to try new things, and that's how he'd had the courage to ask Roxie out when they were on the side of the road. She was probably scared, but she'd still said yes.

"Do you want to share like we used to? Or are you okay without sushi."

He blinked, pulling himself out of his thoughts. "I think I'd like to share. You know?"

"I know."

"I was glad that you asked me out that night," she said once they had divvied up a few pieces of their meal for each other and began eating. "I mean, in a horror film or some thriller book that probably would have been the serial killer on the side of the road with me, but I took a chance with the hot guy who knew what to do with a wrench, and I said yes."

He almost choked on his rice and shook his head. "I know what to do with a wrench?"

She grinned, and he fell in love with her all over again. He loved that smile. He damn well missed it. It had been far too long since he'd seen it, and he blamed himself for that. And maybe her a little, too. He just blamed the whole situation. But tonight wasn't for blame. Tonight, was for beginnings. Tonight, was for a fresh start. Then they could look back. He just hoped to hell they could look forward.

"Of course, you know what to do with a wrench. You are a mechanic." She said it so primly that anyone else listening would have thought she was indeed talking about just a wrench. But this was Roxie Montgomery-Marshall. He knew exactly what she was talking about.

And it was nice to actually know what was on her mind for once. At least for that moment. It had been way too fucking long.

They laughed, even though some awkward spots came up when they tried to talk about her family. Or his. Because they knew all of those things already. They'd had these talks and conversations on their first and second dates back when they first met.

They had burned hot and fast when they first

began. So hot and fast that things had slipped their mind and, suddenly, everything had changed.

He had fallen for her, fallen for her before he really understood what that feeling in his heart and his gut meant. And given how she'd told it before, she had fallen for him just the same.

But when she got pregnant, when they thought they were going to be parents, they had decided to get married.

And everything had changed.

They were in his truck on the way back to the house when that thought crossed his mind.

"You're thinking about it, aren't you?"

He swallowed hard, risking a glance at her before he took the next turn. "I think about it more than I care to admit sometimes."

"Same."

Hell, this was the most they'd said about the fact that she had been pregnant when they got married. They didn't have to say what *it* was. They both knew. And they hadn't talked about it on purpose before. Because it hurt too much.

It hurt right then, too. "I'm glad we went out tonight."

Carter pulled into the driveway and nodded. "Me, too."

They weren't going to talk about it again. They were going to move past that subject. Hopefully, they'd come back to it. And Carter was okay with that. Because he wasn't ready to talk, at least not about what had happened.

But they had to discuss it. Both of them had to get through whatever was blocking them and just deal with it. But first...first, they had to take these next few steps. And a date, even with the awkward parts, was one. And they were damn well doing it.

"I'm going to walk you in, is that okay?"

"I don't think you've ever let me walk to my front door on my own before."

"I guess that is true."

He helped her out of the truck, his hands lingering on her hips. He knew that was a mistake, but he missed her. He always missed her.

When he walked her inside, and she closed the door behind them, they just looked at each other. This was the end of the date, the end of a first.

If it had been any other woman, if it had been a different situation, Carter would have leaned his head down just a little bit to brush his lips along hers.

But he was afraid of what would happen if he did.

"I had fun tonight," she said, her voice raspy.

"So did I. I was afraid it wouldn't be, and that scared me a bit."

She half-laughed like he did. "I know what you mean. I was afraid we weren't going to talk to each other at all and would just sit there in silence. Or I was afraid that we would talk so much that I wouldn't be able to get out of my chair."

"We talked a little. But I think we need to talk more."

"Only not tonight. I hope that's okay. This was a lot all at once."

He gave her a tight nod and then leaned forward, brushing his lips across her cheek. It wasn't the first time he had done that, he just needed to taste her, even if it was just her cheek. But then she tilted her head and brushed her lips along his. He froze, heat scorching his system at that bare touch. Damn it to hell, he missed her.

"I missed you," he whispered.

"I missed you, too." His heart practically shook, rattling between his lungs in his ribcage. Because he had needed to hear those words. He needed so much from her.

This was a step. They were all steps, albeit small. But at least they were fucking taking them. Finally.

"I miss everything that we used to have, but I don't

miss how it ended. And so, I don't want to lead us to a place where that's going to happen again." He nodded at her words, and she continued. "So, that's why I'm not going to ask you upstairs to our bedroom."

He froze, noting the fact that she said *our. Their* bedroom. Not just *hers*. Another step.

"I don't think we should have sex on the first date. Though we did on our real first date."

He smiled with her, but he knew it didn't reach his eyes, just like it didn't really reach hers.

"I think we have a few more steps to take before we're ready for that. The sex was never the problem between us."

"Believe me, that's the one thing we always got right. But I missed this. I missed going out to dinner and sharing my meal with you. I missed talking about the time we first met. Maybe it's a start for something more."

He shook his head. "It's not maybe. It is. I want to take you out again. I want to spend time with you, I just want to be with you. Can you do that? Can we date? Because when we date, we can ask the questions and figure out who we are separately and together. We can talk. Because I think we need to talk."

"We've both said that a few times. I know we need to talk. I just...this is a lot already."

He wiped a tear from her cheek and then kissed her lips again, doing his best to ignore the little clutch of heat in his belly.

"I'll text you to see when we both have time. I know this is your busy time of year, but I want to take you out again. Maybe you can take me out cross-country skiing."

She smiled then, and it reached her eyes. "You would hate it."

"That is probably true. I'm not a huge fan of the snow, but if you like it, I would try it."

"If you want, maybe on our fourth or fifth date."

Damn it to hell. Now that was a step.

And so he kissed her again, knowing that it could be fleeting. Because they hadn't talked about the big things. They had mentioned it in passing, though the fact that they'd even thought of the baby in the same space had to count for something.

And she had said yes to a date, had mentioned more than one. So, Carter was going to take that to heart. And as he walked back to his truck, he didn't have a spring in his step, but he had a clutch in his head. The one that told him that he was going to be okay. Because he had to be.

And because they had to be.

He just knew that the hard stuff was coming, the

part that would likely break them both. And if they got to that step—no, *when* they got to that step—that would be the determining factor of what happened next.

And Carter was just afraid that a first date, even as good as it had been, wouldn't be enough. After all, it hadn't been before.

CHAPTER FOURTEEN

Second dates were different than first ones, but *second*-second dates were different than anything.

Roxie had done this before, she had been on a date with her husband. She had even been on a date with her husband recently. This is just a second date. A *second*-second date.

And if she kept telling herself that, she would probably stress out even more.

But Carter was on his way to pick her up, and they were going ice skating. *Ice skating* of all things. He enjoyed it but had learned as an adult rather than a child. And she had learned when she'd been just a little girl, flailing around as her dad held her hands above her, trying to make sure she didn't fall. The two of them had ended up falling more than once. She was truly surprised that she hadn't cut her dad with those skates of hers.

There was still video of her looking so triumphant right before she fell, her legs going one direction, her arms going another. And the whole time, her dad was trying to keep her up, falling on his butt right at the same time she did. Her father did not have fond memories of ice skating with her and had only done it twice before he gave up and told Shep to do it with her.

She didn't mind, she was really bad at ice skating.

But she had gotten better, had learned not to tilt her skates to the side and actually use her legs the way she was supposed to.

She didn't own her own skates, not like she owned her own skis for cross-country skiing. But Carter didn't own his either, so they planned to rent some at the local rink and skate in circles with the other couples and small children, trying to enjoy their day.

It was probably a weird second date for most people, but it was something they had enjoyed doing back in the day. Okay, so they'd only done it two or three times, but it had made them smile and laugh. They had both fallen on top of each other more than once, but she was pretty sure he had tugged her on top of him. She only knew that because she had made sure to tug him down on her once or twice, too.

She smiled at the memory, at the fact that he had mock scowled at her for daring to pull him down to her level.

So, they weren't the best ice skaters, but they weren't the worst either.

"I'm going to be fine. I'm going to be fine."

Everything would be fine.

Carter rang the doorbell, and Roxie held back a wince. She wished he could just walk in like he had countless times before. But they were setting boundaries with each other as they learned each other again.

The fact that they had mentioned on their date the week before even the concept of what had started to break them apart meant that they were taking steps. Roxie missed the baby they'd never had more than she could breathe, but she and Carter hadn't really talked about it. But she knew they would have to talk about it soon. They were also going to have to talk about everything else surrounding it, and all the things that they had refused to talk about because it had been too hard.

But she was ready. Or at least as ready as she was going to be. She made her way to the door and opened it with a smile on her face.

Carter was there, looking as handsome as ever in

dark jeans and a dark grey Henley long-sleeved shirt. The bomber jacket he wore was open so she could see the way his sweater clung to him.

She loved him in a Henley shirt.

Like, seriously loved him in one. It was a little embarrassing how much she loved him in one. And she remembered tearing it off of him so she could jump on top and have her way with him more than once.

And there she went, thinking about how she missed sex with her husband rather than everything else that they needed to do. But she really missed sex with her husband.

"Are you ready to go ice skating with me, Miss Roxie?" He asked the question with a smile, but she knew he was as tentative as she was.

Their first date had started off awkwardly, even though they had both tried so hard not to make it so. Roxie still thought it was a step in the right direction. It had been a good date, though maybe not as good as her previous dates with him where nothing had been hard, and everything had been easy.

But then again, maybe they needed hard right now. Maybe they needed to work for it this time.

Because they hadn't the first time, and they'd failed because they hadn't realized what they would need to do when times got tough.

"I'm ready. Although I really hope that they give me the correct skates this time. Remember when I skated with two left skates and didn't realize it?"

Carter shook his head. "Well, the skates they have at the rink pretty much all look the same, so I'm surprised we even noticed at all."

"I kept skating in circles, I thought it was me."

"Well…"

"Oh, shut up. It was totally me, too. But let's not talk about that. Let's pretend that I'm totally not going to fall on my ass more than once tonight."

Carter looked down, and she knew that he was probably only pretending not to look at her ass just then, but he was still angling his head just enough to catch a glimpse of it.

She narrowed her eyes at him. "I'm not wearing extra padding back there, so let's be sure not to let me fall too many times."

His eyes grew dark. "Are you saying you're not wearing any underwear?"

She blushed then and wondered why she was blushing when her husband was saying things like that. Of course, it had been far too long since they had joked like this. "I'm wearing normal bikini panties and not a thong because I am wearing jeans, and the idea of that cold ice hitting me sounds horrible."

"I'm surprised you're not wearing leggings, that way, you have more movement."

They were walking to his vehicle, and when he put his hands on her hips to help her into the truck, she put her hands on top of his and met his gaze. She hadn't known how sensual it could be to get into a truck with him. Of course, she had ignored that for far too long, too.

"I needed the extra warmth because I know I'm going to fall. And it's not like I really need the extra movement to like do any tricks or anything. It's going to be hard enough for me to remain upright."

"Well, I'll probably be falling with you, so don't worry about that."

He winked and then shut the door before walking around the truck to get into the cab on the other side.

Falling with you.

They had fallen together before, in more ways than one. And they were doing this. They were talking to each other. Maybe not about the important stuff yet, but that was right under the initial layer. The fact that they were even asking how they were doing and talking about things other than telling each other they would be home late from work was a step in the right direction. They had already spoken to each other more in these past two days than they had in probably the last month of their marriage.

And that was just sad.

"I didn't ask before, but are you going to be okay ice skating with your burns? We can go do something else." She reached out and put her hand on his arm, and he looked down quickly at where she touched him before his eyes went back to the road.

"I'm doing okay, I even asked my doctor if I was allowed to do this, but my skin is all healed up. When they first got me into the surgical room, they were worried that it was third-degree burns, that's why all the staff was as worried as they were. Hell, I bet that's why all of the Montgomerys were as worried as they were."

"It was scary. I really thought it was the end."

He reached out and gripped her hand, and he didn't let it go. She tangled her fingers with his and gave his hand a squeeze.

"I'm okay, Roxie. And Thea is okay, too. We're both okay."

"And I'm glad for that. You saved my sister's life, and I'm never going to forget that. No matter what."

He squeezed her hand again. "And Thea's bakery is back up and running, and one day soon, she'll have her expansion, and everything will be fine. But, as for the scars on my legs and arms, and the one on my side... they're fine. I can work out like I normally do, I can even go swimming now, though I'm not going to want to do that anytime soon because it's cold as hell out there. But ice skating won't be a problem. It's not like I'm going speed skating or playing hockey with someone where I'm just going to slam into them all the time."

"I don't know, do you remember us ice skating? We could be falling on top of each other more than once."

He grinned at her, and she grinned back.

"I think I can handle you landing on top of me," he said with a wink, and she rolled her eyes.

"We're really good about bringing up sex in every single situation, aren't we?"

"It's sort of what we did. A lot. But I can hold myself back. Barely."

She snorted, but she was right there with him. It was really hard not to want her husband. It was just hard to be around him in different ways, but she was going to cherish this time, even if they failed at reconciliation. She would cherish it.

They got to the rink and picked out their skates. Thankfully, Roxie had a left one and a right one, the same as he did. Somehow, they wobbled their way out to the ice after Carter double-checked that her skates were tight enough that they wouldn't fall off. It almost happened only once, but now it was a thing.

As soon as they got on the ice, she put one foot out and almost slid on her butt.

She met Carter's gaze and narrowed her eyes. "Do not laugh."

"Oh, I'm really not going to laugh at that. Because you know I'm going to fall as soon as you do. In fact, let's not even jinx it. Because I'm going to be bruised and black and blue after today, but it'll be worth it. We actually do like ice skating. Even though we're on the ice more than we are upright."

She grinned as he got on the ice, wobbly as her, and they held hands as they did the same circle with everybody else. Some people were going fast around them, moving with grace and agility. Fathers were holding their little girls as the little girls wore helmets. Roxie really wished she would have had a helmet back then, but almost thirty years ago, there wasn't that type of requirement for safety.

She had probably rattled a few things loose with how many times she had fallen.

"My poor father."

Carter laughed as they made the curve. "I remember you telling me that. And then I remember Shep telling me about the fact that he had to take over and ended up with more bruises than he'd gotten when he learned to skate."

"My brother is a bully. And you know he enjoyed skating with me."

"Yes, it probably gave him tips for how to teach Livvy to ice skate."

"Oh my God, just the idea of little Livvy or Daisy in little skates and maybe a little tutu... Oh, I really hope they learn how to ice skate soon."

"I'm sure Mace, Adrienne, and Shep and Shea will take the girls out soon. I think Shep was saying that the girls didn't want to yet because they were having too much fun sledding or something."

They were talking like they were a family, a normal married couple on a normal date. She really liked it. Because they hadn't had that recently. Everything had been so strained, enough that everybody kept watching them and waiting for them to make a move. It was nice to be surrounded by people who didn't know them, who didn't want to make sure that everything was just right, and tip-toeing around them just like they were tip-toeing around each other.

Today was nice.

Roxie knew the hard part was coming, but today... today was nice.

They only fell twice, and she counted that as a win.

Of course, both times it had been her fault, but neither of them mentioned that.

"I swear I'm more graceful on skis than I am on ice skates."

Carter laughed as he parked in her driveway. "Oh, yeah, same here."

"But are you really graceful on skis?"

He put his hand on her shoulder and shoved just slightly. "You're mean."

"I am. But I'm still telling the truth."

"Yeah, whatever. I didn't ask, did you want something to eat? I know we had a snack and hot cocoa at the rink, but that really doesn't constitute dinner."

"Well, thanks to my sister, I have the makings for a nice charcuterie plate with a selection of cheeses. They should still be good. So, some cheese and crackers, maybe a glass of wine? How about that?"

Her stomach turned and went all warm and bubbly as she looked at him, waiting for his answer. He reached across the cab of the truck and cupped her face before brushing his lips along hers. "I'd like that a lot. You know cheese is my downfall."

"I think it's sort of like the number one rule for our group. You have to like cheese. Maybe not to the extent that Thea and Dimitri do, but..."

"I honestly don't think *anyone* could love cheese as

much as they do. It's like a sickness. I mean, who picks a football team because of their love of cheese?"

Roxie laughed as the two of them made their way into the house, still laughing as they made the cheese plate and opened up a bottle of red wine. *This is nice*, she told herself. This was exactly what they needed.

The softness before everything changed.

It hadn't even been like this the first time. Because the first time they hadn't had the hardness under that first layer of goodness.

They hadn't had the past that warred with their present.

But this was nice.

"Okay, so I think the Havarti is my favorite, but this smoked Gouda is amazing."

She rubbed her tummy at Carter's words and leaned into him. They were both sitting on the floor, the cheese plate on the coffee table as they finished up their meal and polished off the half bottle of wine she'd had on the counter.

"I'm sort of in love with everything that's cheese-worthy, but I'm so full now. I cannot believe that was just the leftover cheese in your fridge."

"I bet the next time Thea comes over, my fridge will be full again. I'm very spoiled that way."

"I guess it comes from being the baby of the family."

"I don't mind that. Not at all."

"I can see that." He played with her hair and met her gaze. "Do you remember the first time?"

"The first time?"

"Our first time. Yes, it was our first date, or maybe it was the second. Because I always like to think of the time I fixed your tire as our first date."

"Oh, really? That stressful time where I was trying not to freak out about my tire, and you were on your hands and knees helping me fix it? That was a date?"

"It was the first time I saw you. The first time we talked, and you gave me your number. I'd like to think of that as the first."

"Maybe I might think about it like that, too."

"So then, on our second date, I took you out to dinner and a movie, and then I took you here, right to this living room where we sat down and talked."

"And then we weren't talking anymore."

She swallowed hard, her palms turning clammy.

"I've missed you, Carter."

"I missed you, too." He ran his hands through her hair, his thumb drawing a line along her jaw. "I don't remember the last time we were together. Is that bad? Because it has to be bad."

"I don't remember either." That was a lie. She

remembered, and she had a feeling he did, too. It was just the when of it that was a little cloudy.

"We got so caught up making sure that our businesses were working, so involved in pretending that everything was okay when it wasn't, that we just stopped. We just stopped being with each other, and then we stopped *being* who they were each other."

His words hit home, and Roxie leaned into his shoulder, inhaling his scent. Her hands were on his chest, his warm Henley beneath her skin. She truly loved this shirt.

"Do you ever wish we would've had a bigger wedding?" Carter asked, his voice soft.

She started, and then looked up at him. "No, I was never the girl who thought of the huge dress and the hundreds of people watching me. I always just wanted to be with my family and the man I loved. I never really thought about the china patterns or anything else special like that. I just wanted it to be."

He nodded and cupped her face again. "I was always afraid that we had moved too fast, that I didn't give you what you wanted."

She shook her head quickly. "We got married as quickly as we did because we wanted to. Yes, the circumstances might've made us think we were pushing, but we were all in it no matter what. And, I had the exact day I wanted. I had my family, I had a simple dress, and I had you. It was all I needed."

"Good. I probably should've asked you that before. But I was just afraid that you resented that you didn't get the big weddings that Thea and Adrienne will probably have."

"I never resented it. And I'd like to say I would've told you if I did, but we both know that we weren't very good at talking with each other. We're doing better now than we did throughout the entire year we were together I think."

"I'm glad we are."

"Me, too."

"And, you were right," Carter said softly, "I wanted to marry you before we found out about the baby. I had the ring with me, I was ready to go. The idea that you were pregnant just sort of pushed it into my head that I needed to ask right away. But then again, it also made me think, well, what was I waiting for? You know?"

Her heart warmed, and she nodded. "You told me that when you asked me to marry you. You said you'd had the ring for weeks, even though we'd only been together for a few months. If that."

"And I told you the truth. I'd already been thinking about it, no matter how quickly our courtship went."

"It's just everything that happened after."

She didn't have to say anything more, she didn't want to. They were already talking enough, so when Carter kissed her, she leaned into him and deepened the kiss.

"I don't want to talk anymore," she whispered.

"So, what do you want to do then?"

"You know." She bit his jaw, and his eyes darkened even more.

He wrapped her hair around his fist and tugged, just a little so it hurt, but it still felt so good. He deepened the kiss even more, and she nipped at his lips, her tongue tangling with his. She missed his taste, missed his kisses.

He was such a good kisser. So good with his tongue.

He was just so good at everything, it was hard to keep up sometimes.

But she pushed those thoughts from her head because that had nothing to do with her or him. They were just thoughts that would get in the way of what they were doing right then, and what they might do in the future.

Because this was different. Everything they had done so far was different. They were being open. Honest.

She wanted him. "Make love to me. Make love to me

in the same place we did the first time. Right on this floor in my living room in front of the fire."

"I can do that. I want to do that so badly. But if we do this, it can't be the end. We can't change how we've been talking to each other. And I know that makes me sound like a pussy, but I don't give a fuck."

"I thought you liked pussy," she said, winking.

He laughed then, so hard that he shook against her. "I like your pussy." A pause. "And I miss your pussy."

"Now, with those words, why don't you play with it?"

He laughed again and then sealed his mouth to hers. Soon, he was tugging at his Henley and pulling up her shirt. They moved the wine glasses and coffee table out of the way, and he pulled the blanket down to the floor so she was safely on top of it, cushioned, and he was nestled between her thighs. They kissed, slowly and leisurely.

They already knew each other, but this was getting to know each other once again.

This was her getting to know the pains of his body, the new scars on his arm and his side. She hiccupped a sob as she touched those scars, and then he lifted up so she could kiss them softly, trying to heal them with just her mouth.

Then he met her gaze, and they kissed again, soft and smooth and needing.

They undid each other's pants, and then she was laying down under him in just her bra, bikini panties, and him in his boxer briefs. She could see the scar on his leg, and she ran her calf against it, soothing it.

He said it didn't hurt anymore, but he had fallen on that side on the rink, and she knew he would bruise. But he had still gone out that day, just for her.

Or, maybe, for them. Roxie wouldn't forget that.

Her stomach clenched, and she arched up into him as he slowly undid her bra, kissing between the valley of her breasts. And then his mouth went to her nipple before going to the other.

She gasped, out of breath as he plucked and sucked at her. Cupping her breasts in his hands, he pressed them together so he could kiss them at the same time.

He'd always loved her breasts, much like he loved her ass. He was forever kissing and touching and molding her. She had missed this so damned much.

They were learning each other again, not just their emotions, not just the memories, but each other's bodies.

Sex was an important part of their relationship but had never been the only thing. But, at one point, it had been the thing that they could rely on when nothing else worked.

So, the fact that they were trying to make everything else work and then coming to this, that meant everything.

They were going to make this work.

And then, all thoughts were gone when he slowly slipped her panties down her legs and put his mouth between her thighs.

She gasped, tangling her fingers in his hair as he sucked on her pussy. His fingers played with her clit, and then her lower lips. He was doing exactly what he had done in her dream, and she couldn't help but whisper his name as she came, her legs clamping down on his shoulders as he continued to eat her out, sucking up her orgasm.

She hadn't come that quickly in years. But, apparently, she needed him. She always needed him. And then, he was over her, and she was helping him slide off his boxer briefs.

He was hard and ready, moisture glistening at the tip. She gripped him, and he groaned. And then, she met his gaze as she ran her thumb over the slit on the top of his dick, spreading the moisture around.

"I've missed this," she said, giving him a squeeze.

"I've missed this so damned much."

"I've missed all of this. All of you. This isn't the end," Carter promised. "This is only the beginning."

Maybe those words would've sounded cheesy to someone else, but not to her, not between them. This was just the two of them. Only them. Yes, their past and their present and even their future was all around them, but right then, it was just him and her.

Because she was still on birth control, and they were both still clean, he slid into her, no questions asked, none needed.

Because she trusted him, she trusted that he hadn't touched that other woman when they weren't together. And he trusted her because she had told him that she hadn't been with another man.

Trust had never been the problem between them. It was trusting themselves that was the issue.

It was trusting their own worth to and with each other. He slid into her, hard and slow, and she ached.

"So tight," he whispered and groaned.

"I think it's because you're too big," she whispered, squeezing him internally.

Carter hovered above her and then took her lips in a daunting kiss. "You always say the best things to me."

And then he moved. Her hands were going down his back, gently moving over his scars as he slid in and out of her. She wrapped her legs around his waist, arching into him.

They were moving as one, moving as if they had never been apart, and yet they had been apart just long enough to miss each other to the point of breaking.

She could feel every single pull of him, every single inhale and exhale. And then she came, and he followed, filling her with heat and his need.

And then the two of them were holding each other, still locked together as one as they lay on the floor of the living room, the same place they had first made love.

The very place she had fallen for him.

And then, they just held each other, no words needed.

Because the words would come, and they'd get through the hard parts.

But there had to be a light at the end of the tunnel.

And this...this was part of it.

She loved the man holding her, and she knew he loved her.

And not just because of the sex, not just because of what she was feeling right then, but because of everything. She thought that love could maybe be enough.

Maybe she could find that hope.

Maybe she was holding him, after all.

CHAPTER FIFTEEN

Almost a month of dating his wife meant a month of learning new things about the two of them. And Carter was actually enjoying himself more than he thought possible.

He shouldn't have been surprised though, because before they stopped talking, before they stopped being who they needed to be for each other, they had always enjoyed their time together.

They had always gone on dates, used whatever spare time away from both of their long hours of work so they could just be with one another.

They were friends, they always had been. And, somehow, that had gotten lost in it all. But Carter was glad that they were figuring it out. Together. Tonight, however, tonight he was going to enjoy himself again.

He was going to go out with the woman he loved, and they were going to have dinner, see a movie, maybe go on a walk, and perhaps do something more. He and Roxie had only slept together twice in the weeks they'd been dating again. That first time had been so unromantic, neither had been able to speak let alone fully comprehend what it meant for them.

But they had talked for the rest of that evening, though he hadn't spent the night.

Neither of them was ready for that. Maybe if he didn't still have some of his stuff there, or if he didn't actually have his name on the deed. Or if he hadn't lived there, it wouldn't have been a problem. But even though they had slept together on their second date, they were still taking things slowly. So, he hadn't spent the night, and he hadn't spent the night the second time they slept together either. That time, it had been hard and fast against the door in her bedroom, and then he had bent her over the edge of the bed, fucking her hard until they both came screaming each other's names. He hadn't spent the night, but he had stayed long enough to go at it again, this time slow with him behind, slowly pumping in and out of her.

They had gone achingly slow, surprisingly sweet.

There hadn't been anything awkward about it.

None of the times they came together since reconnecting had been awkward.

And he knew that wouldn't always be the case. Awkward sex was sometimes some of the best sex, in real couples and real-life situations.

But for now, they were Roxie and Carter again.

Only a different kind. The kind that actually spoke to one another and tried to stop hiding what they were feeling for fear of hurting one another. No, they weren't completely done with the ghosts of their past, but they were working their way through them.

And it counted more than not.

Once again, Carter pulled his truck into the driveway and looked up at the house he had once lived in. He would love to move back in, would love to be in her life for more than just a date a week or just texting every day and phone calls. But they were getting closer, that much he knew.

Though there was one major thing they needed to discuss, one thing they needed to make sure they could pull through before they could move forward. And they were getting closer to being able to talk about it, but there were so many other things on the docket, they seemed to be pushing that down. Maybe it was to protect themselves, or maybe it was because they knew they would miss everything else if they talked about that first. Because it wasn't just the big things, it was the little things, too. And he had learned the hard way not to ignore anything.

He hopped out of his truck and rubbed his hands together. It was still way too damn cold for late March and nearing spring in Colorado. Although, knowing his state, it would snow up until June with random ninety-degree days in the middle. It never eased in to nice weather. It was always sudden, intense, or a little bit of snow thrown in to remind you that winter was just around the corner.

Carter just hoped that tonight wouldn't be too cold for a walk.

Because Roxie loved walking in the park, and he wanted to make sure they could do it again.

This time when Roxie opened her door, she was laughing, a smile on her face, wearing the skin-tight black dress that she had worn when they were together that always made his cock spring to action. He almost growled. She had long sleeves, and tights again, along with those black boots that he loved. They cupped her calves, and he knew that he'd love stripping them off of her.

Damn, if he was lamenting and waxing poetic about her boots, he was officially losing his mind.

"What's so funny?" he asked as he walked inside, laying a kiss on her lips.

"I was just on the phone with Shep, and he was telling me a story about Livvy and jam and honey. Apparently, they have a joke about jam hands that I don't really get, but I think it's from a TV show."

Carter snorted. "Oh, yeah, I know that joke. It's like when all kids, no matter what you do, always end up with sticky hands. Even with no jam in the house. None in the vicinity, they still end up with jam hands. Sticky fingers that end up touching your face. Your hair. Jam everywhere."

"Well, there was jam in his beard, jam in his hair, and it's not like he is a little toddler anymore."

"It doesn't matter until they are eighteen and out of the house. If there is a will, there will be jam."

"I think I need to ask my mom to stitch that onto a pillow for him. Shep would probably get a kick out of it."

"Or you could try to do it."

"Do you remember me sewing? Do you remember me knitting? Adrienne at least is decent at it. I am not good at art. I noticed."

He shook his head and helped her to the truck again, this time giving her a hard kiss as he helped her into the cab. He closed the door and made his way to the other side and into the driver's seat so he could finish the conversation without losing his thoughts.

"You need to stop giving yourself a hard time about that art thing. You are brilliant."

"You're just saying that because you want to get under this dress."

"One, of course, I want to get under that dress. But me telling you that you are brilliant has nothing to do with that."

"Sure."

"No, you are brilliant. And it's not that you don't know you're brilliant. Because I know you do."

"Now you're just confusing me."

"Maybe, but that's because I'm not using the right words. You are so damn smart, Roxie. And talented. Just because you don't paint like your sisters or knit or any of the other physical crafty things they do, doesn't mean you don't have talent. It's just that your talents lie in other areas. You've always beat yourself up about that. And I've never liked it, but I've never known how to tell you that I believe in you. I think the art that you bring home from that Brushes with Lushes is beautiful. I would totally put it on our wall if you let me. Because it's something you did. It's something you created. I can't do that. I've tried. And I'm not saying that to try and make you feel better or try to make *me* feel better about not being able to do it. It's just something that doesn't happen. And just because your sisters can do some things differently, doesn't mean that your worth is of any less value."

He didn't have to say all of that, but the words had just sprung out of him. He should have said all of those things long ago because it wasn't like Roxie feeling inadequate when it came to art was anything new. It had been something under the surface since before he even met her.

And though he had tried to say the right words, they had never come out right.

As she wiped the tears from her cheeks, he was really afraid that he had made the wrong move once again.

"I'm sorry. I shouldn't have said that."

"No, you should have. I'm just...I just..." She took a breath. "You should have said it. I'm glad you did."

He pulled in to the parking lot of the movie theater and hoped he wasn't too much of an idiot. "I'm sorry, Roxie."

"No, don't be sorry. I know I have this stupid thing going on in my head where I think I need to compete with my sisters and my family about what we do with art. And it's because they are all so amazing with their talents that, sometimes, I wonder why I didn't get that gene."

"But you're not bad."

"Thanks."

He winked.

"You know what I meant."

"I do. And I know I'm not bad at it. I know it just takes me longer, and I have to think about it differently. I just put so much into it that I sometimes do stupid things. And I put myself down because of it."

"And that's okay. I mean, it's not okay that you put yourself down, I didn't mean that."

"I know," she said with a laugh.

"It's more the fact that it's okay that you don't do things the same as your family. You know they don't like numbers the way you do. And you know that they don't like cross-country skiing like you do. Although, Liam does. I need to meet this Liam."

This time, she rolled her eyes. "You know he's my cousin, right?"

"I did not know that when the girls mentioned that you were going skiing with this Liam. It took them a little too long to explain to me that, yes, he's your cousin from Boulder. I was really jealous."

She gave him a look as they walked into the movie.

"Jealous? You're the one who went on a date with someone else."

"Jesus Christ. I'm so sorry I did that."

They were going to a matinee because they didn't like going to packed movie theaters, and later they wanted to go to dinner. And because of that, there was no one else around for this conversation. Thank God.

"No, I really shouldn't have brought up the date because it doesn't bother me. I know it should, but in the end, it brought you to my doorstep. It brought you to me to say the words that you needed to say and finally got me off my ass to say the words *I* needed to. So, I can't really be too angry about those words. I can't be angry about that date. I know I should be, and I know that someone you worked with still knows this woman, and I know that we may see her at a grocery store one day. But I promise I will not rip her face off with my nails. Because you sitting with someone else for a meal and not touching them at all brought you to me. And it opened up your heart a bit so you could speak to me again. That way, I could speak to you. And I'm okay with that. Even if I may growl a bit and bring it up just to joke around. You're welcome to bring up the mysterious Liam if you want."

He rolled his eyes and then kissed the top of her head, relieved that she felt that way. He knew that she had talked with Kaylee about the other woman seeing him with Stacia too, and the two of them were just fine with each other. He had been afraid that Kaylee holding back like she had would hurt her relationship with Roxie, but in the end, honesty was the best policy.

He had never once lied to his wife, he just hadn't spoken to her the way he should.

And he was going to be better about that.

Damn it.

They settled in for their movie with their small popcorn and soda to share. Neither of them was a big fan of either of those things, but you couldn't go to a movie without both.

They cuddled and watched the movie in silence, even though there weren't that many people in the movie theater with them. In fact, if they wanted to, they probably could have made out like teenagers, but they were adults. They had standards, after all. A little bit anyway.

"You know, anything with a bearded Chris Hemsworth makes me happy."

"You mean the part with the shirtless Chris Hemsworth, don't you?" he asked as they finished up their meals at one of their favorite restaurants.

"Well, that is true, and though I really didn't understand the movie, it was brilliant.

It was one of the first movies he had seen recently that wasn't an actual superhero movie. Usually, he only liked to go to superhero movies in the theater these days. He was becoming an old man and didn't like to hold his bladder for anything but a superhero.

Roxie had always said she didn't like to hold her bladder for anything but one of the Chrises.

He oddly wasn't jealous about that because they were hot. He didn't blame her.

"So, Mr. Marshall, what're your plans for the rest of the evening?" Roxie asked as they walked hand-in-hand to the park. "Because I have to say, you're pretty much hitting all the romantic buttons at this point."

He tugged her close, tucked her under his arm and to his side, and kissed her hard and fast. "I like the fact that you think that. Makes me feel like I'm doing the right thing."

"You were always pretty smooth at that. I'm enjoying this side of you, the one that's smiling and just being."

He held her hand again and continued to walk, grateful there weren't too many people out and about since it was still a bit chilly. But they were wrapped up, and so he hoped that neither of them would get sick.

"Toward the end there, I was focused so much on

work and keeping my place afloat, I felt like I was failing. You know?"

"I was working just as hard, just as many hours. It's hard when you're young and not exactly struggling anymore, but maybe struggling for the next step. Because we could pay our mortgage, our bills weren't the problem. It was that next level of what we were both fighting for, and in doing so, we kind of ignored everything else."

"It was easier to put ourselves into work than what actually mattered."

"Our work does matter. We can't push that aside."

"Neither of us are. I know you're in the middle of tax season, but the fact that you can actually take a few hours each week with me...I appreciate it."

"I think I was going crazy last year. For more than one thing, but during tax season and not being able to actually relax? That was stupid of me, and I got that horrible cold because of it."

"I remember. You wouldn't even let me give you some chicken noodle soup."

"It's because I like the chicken and stars."

"I know, I even bought extra cans of it just for you."

"And I was so far into my head wanting to make sure that I could do everything on my own, that I didn't let you make it for me."

"So, if you get sick tonight while we're taking this walk, are you going to let me feed you some chicken and stars?"

"I think that can be arranged. But let's just stay huddled together so we don't catch a cold."

"Sounds good to me." They continued walking a bit, talking about the weather and her family some more. Carter was talking about Landon and the fact that he and Kaylee were still not actually dating yet. That made her laugh, and he kissed the tip of her nose, noticing that it was getting a bit chilly. They would have to head in soon, but he didn't want this night to end.

"Back to that work thing. There're other reasons I forced myself to work as hard as I did." He didn't say the words too loudly since other couples were walking along the path now, but she stopped where she was and tugged him close so she could focus on him.

"Why, Carter? Talk to me."

"It's stupid, really."

"It's not stupid if you felt that way. So, tell me."

"You're going to think I'm silly." He ran his hand over his hat, forgetting that he couldn't run his fingers through his hair because of it. Then he gave her a chagrined smile before starting again. "I told you you're brilliant, and that's true. All of your family is. You've all gone to special schools or college or even got your master's degrees in some cases. You are so fucking brilliant. Sometimes, I forget that I'm the mechanic, the guy on the outside looking in. I'm the one who's not quite bright, not quite as white-collar as you guys."

"Carter."

"I know it's stupid. I know that I own a business. And I know that your family's full of tattoo artists and construction workers. You guys are bakers and people who work with your hands. You're artists. But you're a fucking accountant, and you're so brilliant and so much...more. Sometimes, I just feel a little stupid. But that's not on you."

"I hope not. I hope I never did anything to make you feel like you were stupid."

"You never did. That's all on me. And I know I shouldn't feel that way. But, sometimes, I couldn't help it."

"Like sometimes I can't help but compare myself to my sisters and their art?"

"Pretty much. And I know it's just something inherent in people how they have to compare themselves to others and find their own inadequacies even if they aren't there. But sometimes I felt like I had to struggle to keep up and make sure my business was always staying afloat so I wasn't the one pulling you down."

"Carter. That's ridiculous. I probably shouldn't have used that word because, if you felt it, then it's not really ridiculous, it's something that is rooted somewhere deep. And you said I never made you feel that way, not really, but I'm going to do my best to make sure I never accidentally do. Okay? Because I don't want you to ever feel that you have to compare yourself to me, or that you're less than anything I am. Because we're supposed to lift each other up. Maybe I didn't do that enough for you. Because I remember you trying to make me feel better about my art. I remember, at first, when we were still talking more, that you always put me first. I remember all of that, but I don't think I did enough for you. And that's something that I lack. That's something I need to change. It's something I'm going to change. This is our second chance, Carter. And I don't want to mess it up. I don't want to fall into the same mistakes because we're afraid. So, Carter Marshall, I think you're brilliant. So fucking brilliant. And I love you. I don't want to lose you again."

Carter blinked, making sure he'd heard the words right. He loved her so damn much, and he was afraid, at least he had been afraid that she didn't feel the same way with him. He was afraid that everything they were doing wouldn't end up the way it should. That she would find him lacking in the end or find that it was easier if they weren't together.

"We're going to make this work, Roxie. The two of us. We're going to make this work."

"I know we are. Not because we have to, not only that. Because we want to. I don't want to fall into the same mistakes again."

"So, let's not. Let's work on that." And so they continued to walk, making their way back to his truck and then to the house.

And when they made love in their bed that night, she rode him, his hands on her breasts, her head arched back as she moved her hips. He pumped into her, aching, needing.

And after they came together, they held each other long into the night. He spent the night, actually stayed until morning, holding his wife.

This was another step.

They were going to make it.

No, they weren't finished yet.

But they were getting closer.

In love. Love could be enough.

There was hope.

CHAPTER SIXTEEN

Roxie had loved Montgomery dinners until she learned to hate them. Now, nervousness warred with the anticipation of seeing her family after so long ignoring them. Yes, she'd done some meals with her sisters, and yes, she talked to her family on the phone, but she'd missed every other family dinner and game night until now.

Most of it, honestly, was because of tax season and Roxie using her free time to either get her head on straight with regards to her own well-being when it came to skiing or just sleeping, and the other times were for Carter.

So now here she was, ready to go to her first Montgomery dinner in far too long. And she was going to take Carter with her. She really hoped it wasn't as awkward as she felt it might be.

Because her family loved Carter, they really did. They just hadn't known how to act around him these last few months. And that was on them. She and Carter were still working out exactly who they were in this new relationship of theirs, and the others had actually given them space.

She had honestly been a little surprised that they had, considering it wasn't something they normally did. Her family loved to try and take care of her. They loved to try and take care of each other. Meaning, they were always up in each other's business.

They weren't now, though. They were giving her space.

But today...today would change everything. Today, Roxie was going to dinner at her parents' house. Her sisters and brother would be there, their significant others and children would be there. And Roxie thought Liam might be there too since she had extended the invite directly from her mother on their last skiing trip.

Carter had not come with her for that, mostly because he'd had to work and he had known that he wouldn't be able to keep up with them.

But maybe one day she would take him out, even if

he hated it. Because it was something that they tried to do together.

And then maybe they could find something else that they could do together. Maybe if they actually found things they enjoyed doing as a couple outside of having sex, they would be able to make it work this time. Because before, they had spent so long worrying about making sure they had enough money for the future, making sure they didn't talk about the thing that hurt the most, that they'd sort of ruined everything else they could have had because they buried themselves.

But things were going to get better.

"You ready?" Carter asked as they pulled in to her parents' driveway. Her siblings were already there, their cars parked on the road, but they had left a space for her, and she couldn't help but smile. They had kept the spot for her because they wanted her to know that she was welcome. Or everybody had left the space open for the next arrival, and she was just that person. Knowing her family, it could be either. Or both.

"I'm oddly nervous but ready."

Carter reached over and squeezed her hand. "Same. I just hope your brother doesn't kick my ass."

"He won't. Because he'll have to go through me

first." She looked over at Carter then and kissed him softly on the jaw. He turned off the car and then leaned over to capture her lips.

She sank into him, smiling even as they kissed. She had missed this. She had missed this more than she could possibly imagine. It felt like they were back. Okay, maybe not back, but rather to where they should have been this whole time. She didn't want to overthink it, didn't want to stress herself out over it, but it felt like maybe, just maybe, things would be okay.

So, when the knock on the window came, she screamed against Carter's lips, and her husband laughed, his eyes crinkling at the corners.

"Are you done sucking face? Mom and Dad are watching, you know."

Roxie flipped off Adrienne and then laughed along with Carter as they both got out of the car.

She hugged her sister tightly, as Carter ran around to the back and got the pie.

She hadn't baked it herself since there hadn't been time, but the local bakery by her house was one of her mom's favorites, and the family wouldn't mind that it was store-bought. Because, frankly, it was one of the best pies they could get, other than Thea's.

Nothing was better than Thea's.

And it wasn't Thea's turn to bake the pies this time. You would think that since Thea was the baker of the family, she would always be the one to bring the baked goods, but they made sure that Thea got time off. That left her sister more time to work on her cooking skills, such as the bourbon meatballs Roxie knew would be waiting for her in the house. Well, that and the cheese plates. Nothing could stop Thea and now Dimitri from bringing cheese plates to any party. It was sort of a thing. And it was adorable.

"I'm so glad you're here," Adrienne said after kissing Roxie hard on the cheek. "My little sister's all grown up and bringing her husband and pie that I know she didn't bake."

Roxie rolled her eyes. "Yes, because with all the time I have, I totally could've baked a pie or three."

"You have three pies?"

"We couldn't decide which one to get, so we got all three."

Carter lifted them up as he spoke and grinned. "We got bourbon pecan, this chunky apple with rhubarb in it, and this chocolate pie that I think has salted caramel in it. I'm not a hundred percent sure, but I almost passed out while the woman was describing it."

"Now that sounds like a good pie."

Roxie watched as the two of them interacted, and she was grateful that it sounded as if everything would be okay, or at least not as tense as she'd thought it might be at first. Because Adrienne was doing just fine, and she ran around and took a pie from Carter before giving him a side hug.

Everyone was already inside by the time they got there, but Roxie didn't mind. It had taken Carter an extra thirty minutes to leave the shop because of a dispute with a customer that he'd had to handle himself. She knew that he was doing better about delegating, but sometimes somebody just needed to talk with a manager. And, according to her husband, the customer had been wrong, but they had still made everything work out. She was just glad that they were there now so everything could get started. Maybe after this first meeting, everything would be better. After all, everything was already so much better than it had been even a month ago. Heck, even a week ago.

"You're here," her mom said as she rushed to them. She held Roxie close in a deep hug, kissing her on the forehead before moving to Carter. "And you brought pies. Ms. Nancy's pies. They're not my Thea's, but I still think they're pretty good."

"There's nothing better than my pies, but I don't mind you bringing the competition into the house that we grew up in. I mean, we have to let the others have some chance at true competition, right?" Thea asked, laughing. Her sister might be competitive, but not in the way she was saying. Just the fact that they could joke, and everyone was acting like everything was normal and that nothing was wrong, meant they were all on the right track.

At least, Roxie hoped.

"I'm so glad you're here, Carter. You're looking well."

"I'm doing just fine. The doctor gave me a clean bill of health. I'm still doing my PT exercises because the skin sometimes pinches, but it's just going to be for a while, I think."

Roxie ran her hand down her husband's back as her mom's eyes filled before Mrs. Montgomery blinked them away. And then her mom reached for the pies and kissed Carter smack on the lips.

"I love you, my son. Just in case you didn't know that."

Then her mom walked away, and the others came to hug Carter, and Roxie knew that she wasn't the only one shocked to her core, wasn't the only one feeling as if she had lost her balance. Because her mom had never called Carter, *son*. She hadn't called Dimitri or Mace that either. It wasn't really something their family did, like how Shea didn't call their mother *Mom* or anything like that.

So, it wasn't just a title, it was something that meant connection. And, yes, it was because Carter was back in Roxie's life, but she also knew it was because he had saved Thea's. And that was something you couldn't just walk away from. It was something you didn't just forget.

Roxie's family was connected in more ways than one, and the idea that she was actually trying to be a part of it again, that she wasn't hiding anymore, and that she was facing what she had head-on—at least in some respects—meant she felt like she was growing up.

And growing into her new self with her husband by her side.

Dinner was rambunctious as usual, but she knew it wasn't as boisterous as it was at some of the other family gatherings. In fact, her cousin Liam even commented on that as they were eating.

"Aunt Katherine, I think you may be an even better cook than my mom, but if you ever say I said that, I'll deny it. I swear I will."

Roxie laughed into her napkin while Carter gave her a raised brow. Yes, Carter was still a little miffed by the fact that he had thought Liam was someone she was with rather than just her cousin, but she knew that it was all in jest, so that was just fine. She had an idea that Liam had figured it out too, so he did his best to put his arm around her chair and wink over at Carter.

Roxie was going to pay her cousin back for that later. Maybe when he actually settled down. She hoped it was soon because Liam deserved to be happy, but she also knew better than most that relationships were hard work and sometimes it was okay to breathe before you jumped in.

"So, Carter, how's the shop going?" her dad asked as they finished up their desserts. The pies had been amazing, the chocolate caramel was still settling in her stomach, and she knew if she breathed just right, she could maybe make space for one more piece.

"The shop's doing good. I have to hire on someone else I think and promote one of my guys as another assistant manager—maybe assistant to the assistant or something like that."

Roxie looked over at Carter and smiled. They had talked about that, and she had looked over his books with him since she was still his accountant. It all made sense to them, and she loved that while they weren't expanding the business, he was making sure they could keep up with the high demand.

"That's wonderful. And that reminds me, I need an

oil change on the truck." Her dad frowned, and Roxie just smiled as Carter nodded.

"We can handle that. Just bring it into the shop sometime, and I'll work it into the schedule. I'll handle it myself."

"I would assume nothing less. I mean, I am a Montgomery, I deserve the best." Her dad said it with such an air of superiority that was so unlike him that all of them broke out into laughter.

"Yes, the Montgomerys do deserve the best," Thea said, grinning.

"Yes. The best." Shep glared just a little at Carter, and Roxie knew that out of all the Montgomerys, Shep would probably be the last one to forgive Carter. Then again, there was nothing for her family to forgive or forget. Her relationship with Carter was between her and Carter, and she had tried to make that clear before. If need be, she would do so again.

Because they had both made mistakes, and that meant they had to figure out what they needed to do with each other rather than what the family might think they should do.

They were all sitting in the living room drinking wine or coffee as the dinner wound down. Roxie loved her family, adored the way the little kids had passed out on the floor in front of the fire with the big, old dog cuddling with them. She loved the fact that everybody had paired off, at least everyone but Liam, and were all curled into each other, a huge family that actually liked one another.

Roxie knew it was rare, though she hadn't really known anything but this her whole life. But Shep was back in town, and he was going to stay, and she was going to do better about being part of her family. She wasn't going to run away anymore, wasn't going to hide.

She just had to remember that, when things got tough, she could lean on others.

And the first person she needed to lean on was Carter. Because not speaking to him, not telling him her fears, that was what had hurt him. And him doing the same to her had hurt even more.

She knew they still needed to talk about what they had lost, but they would. Soon.

Liam leaned forward as he continued his conversation, and she pulled herself out of her thoughts so she could focus. "Yes, so I have this cabin up in the woods by my place that I haven't been able to use in the past couple of weeks because of work. It's getting a little ridiculous how much I don't actually use the property I own."

Roxie looked over at her cousin. "A cabin in the

woods? Isn't that just asking for a serial killer to come at you?"

He snorted. "I'm a big, tough man who can wield an ax for firewood. I think I'll be okay."

"You know, that's what the guy who gets killed in the prologue always says."

Liam just grinned at her, and Carter kissed the top of her head. "Are you saying you need someone to go up there and actually use it?" Carter asked, surprising her.

"Yeah, that's what I was going to bring up. I figured you and Roxie could use some time away. And, yes, I'm being pushy. But Roxie knows that I'm pushy when I feel like it."

"What are you talking about?" Roxie asked, leaning forward. "You're saying you want us to go use your cabin for a weekend or something?"

"That's exactly what I'm saying. I figured the two of you could use the time together. And yes, I'm talking about the huge elephant in the room that we're not talking about. However, if you'd like a weekend or a long weekend away from the big, mountainous Colorado Springs and take a walk into the big, mountainous Boulder, you're welcome to use my cabin. And I'm not actually kidding that I could use some help making sure the place is doing okay. I have a caretaker, but they've had a cold for the past couple of days, and I worry that they're not going to be able to check on it soon enough. So, just let me know."

"Is this an open invitation for any of us?" Adrienne asked, grinning. "Because I think that Mace and I could use a vacation, too."

"The place is always open for any Montgomery. Or one of their friends, if you actually trust them. But, really though, Roxie, there's a great place to ski right by there so I know you'd like it. And, Carter, I have a huge garage out there with an old car that I've been working on if you want to look at it. Not that I'd actually let you touch my baby, but you can look at her."

"I don't know if we can make the time," Carter said softly, looking at Roxie.

"It's tax season, it's probably the worst time for me to take a weekend off."

"You should do it," Shea said. "You can take a three-day weekend. I'm going to try and do the same with Shep because we need to go back down to New Orleans for an old client."

That was the first Roxie had heard of it, but she knew that her brother and his wife went down to New Orleans a few times a year to visit their old friends.

"Maybe. Maybe."

Roxie looked at her husband then, and he leaned

down and kissed her softly. "Let's make time. Just you and me."

And though everybody was looking at them, she couldn't help but look into Carter's eyes and nod.

"Okay."

Because they needed time for themselves, even though they had been taking more time than usual. It was time they should've taken forever ago. So, they would take Liam up on his offer and camping. Or at least camping in a cabin, which, knowing her cousin, was probably far more luxurious than her house.

They would take time for each other. And that was all that mattered.

By the time they got home, Roxie was hot for her husband and full of food and promises.

"I want you," she whispered against his lips. They were standing in the foyer, her back to the door, and his hands on her ass.

"Oh, yeah? How much?" He ground his cock against her, and she moaned.

"You know how much." He had her against him, so she wrapped her legs around his waist. The fact that he could hold her up while sucking on her neck and then her breasts, just made her wetter—if that was even possible.

"Let's see how much," he growled. Then he had his fingers under her dress and inside her.

"Jesus Christ," she gasped, her nails digging into his shoulders. "Holy fuck. How did you get around my panties so fast?"

"I've got moves you've never seen." He curled his fingers, hitting her G-spot in one move.

Hell.

She snorted. "Are you really quoting *My Best Friend's Wedding* while you have me on the verge of coming?"

"Maybe. But if you're only on the verge, I'm not doing it right." Then he curled his fingers again, and she saw stars, her inner walls clamping around him as she came, her body shaking against the door.

"So fucking beautiful. I love the way you come."

"I want to see you come, too."

"That can be arranged." He slid his fingers out of her and licked one, his eyes on hers. Her pussy clenched. Then he used the other finger to trace her lips.

So. Sexy.

He kissed her again, and she rocked into him, wanting him even more. She'd missed this, the heat, the need, the everything that came with Carter. When he kissed her neck and let her legs fall to the floor, she wiggled away from him and winked.

"Let me see you come, then."

He raised his brows. "You want me to jack off in front of you?"

She squeezed her legs together because...dear God. That image.

Yes, that would last a long time in her brain.

Like, forever.

"Okay, we can start with that. Take off your shoes and pants, Mr. Marshall. Get to it."

"As long as you take off that dress of yours." His eyes darkened, and she nodded.

"Deal."

They stripped in front of each other, almost tripping as they laughed and kissed in between removing pieces of clothing. Sex with Carter was *fun*. It was hot. It was sweet. It was everything.

And, right then, it meant even more.

When she went to her knees in front of him, his eyes got wide, and he gripped the base of his cock.

"I thought you wanted me to jack off."

"Get squeezing, buddy, I'll just work on your balls here." She licked one and then the other, and he groaned, moving his hand up and down his shaft, using the moisture at the tip to help.

Then she sucked one ball into her mouth, then moved to the other. And when he arched into her, she let him go with a pop, then licked up his cock, kissing his fingers before swallowing the plump head.

"Roxie," he growled as if that were all he could get out. And she didn't mind.

She worked him until he pulled away, and then he was tugging her up, his mouth on hers.

"I wasn't done," she said, nipping at his lip.

"I'm going to come in that pussy of yours. Bend over that table, Rox. Let's fuck." He winked, and she laughed.

"Oh, you're so romantic."

He smacked her ass as she made her way to the dining room table, and she yelped.

"Hey!"

"I'm romantic. So romantic that you're going to come hard on my cock. Nipples to the table, Montgomery-Marshall. Ass in the air."

She had no idea why that turned her on so much, but she eagerly did as he instructed. She bent over and wiggled her ass for him.

"Hop on, Marshall."

He gripped her hip and then smacked her ass again with his other hand. Her pussy pulsated at the hit, and she groaned. "That's my girl."

Then he rubbed away the sting before going to his knees. His mouth was on her in the next instant, and she was pressing her ass to his face, arching for him and coming in less than a minute. The man knew *exactly* what to do with his tongue.

And before she could complain that she'd gotten off twice and he hadn't yet, he was back on his feet and slamming into her with one perfect thrust.

"Yes!" they both called out.

And then he was moving, and she was shouting, and they were both panting, sweating, and aching. He leaned over her, biting her shoulder, kissing her, and running his hand down her back.

She could barely think, could hardly do anything but feel him. And when he came, she called his name again, needing more, just needing him.

He pulled out, cleaned them both up in the kitchen, and carried her to the couch where she curled up in his lap as he covered them both with a blanket.

"It's safe to say," she began after a moment in the warm silence, "that we're never going to be able to eat there again."

He kissed the top of her head. "I don't know, I say I just ate a pretty damn good meal over there just now."

She lazily slapped at his shoulder and smiled, nodding off slightly as he held her, running his hands down her body. This was their new normal, their new *them*.

She knew there was more to come, but for now, this was what they needed.

She loved him.

Loved them.

Loved what they could be and have.

And she promised herself she'd try to keep it.

No matter what.

CHAPTER SEVENTEEN

Roxie knew the Rocky Mountains were beautiful. Hell, she lived in Colorado Springs and practically lived *in* them. But the view from the cabin up in Boulder was like nothing she'd ever seen before.

Beauty in every sense of the word.

Utter breathtaking exquisiteness.

She was so grateful that they'd come up here. That they were going to take time to themselves and just be.

"I can't believe Liam has this place," Carter said as he wrapped his arms around her waist. "It's gorgeous. And I did not realize how much money your cousin had."

Roxie leaned back into him, inhaling his scent, the one that she loved as it mixed with that of the trees and the mountains around her. It was as if they belonged here, even though this was only a temporary stay, and their home was back down south. Back in those mountains.

Yes, all of the mountains around here were the Rockies, and they shared the same foothills, but Roxie knew exactly what her skyline looked like, each peak, the ways she thought one set of peaks looked like a different object versus another. She knew that no matter where she was, she could just look towards the west and see Pike's Peak and know she was home.

She didn't know the names of the peaks up in Boulder. Didn't know the different sight lines. Yes, she had been to Boulder, and to Estes Park and all those other places a few times. You couldn't escape it if you lived in Colorado and actually liked being out in nature.

But this wasn't her home. However, it was a great place to visit.

"I think he's done pretty well with his job amongst other things."

"Are you saying he's some kind of mafia mobster? Maybe even a pirate?"

Roxie snorted and turned in Carter's arms, reaching up onto her tiptoes so she could kiss his jaw. He hadn't shaved, and the stubble had gotten soft. She loved when he had a beard. She could just eat him up.

"Yes, my cousin Liam is a pirate in the mountains. He has a pirate ship that he just rides over the peaks and goes over rolled logs instead of water. It's quite a sight to behold."

They both laughed, and Carter shook his head. "Now I'm actually picturing that and want to see if it could actually happen. Who do we know that could build something like that, even if in miniature?"

"Probably one of the Denver cousins or someone they're married to. That's the construction arm of the family, we're a different set down in Colorado Springs."

Carter looked around, nodding. "It seems Liam and his siblings are a different set completely up in Boulder."

"Just wait until you meet the Ft. Collins Montgomerys."

Carter shuddered. "There are so many of you guys. Sometimes, it's actually a little overwhelming."

"That's why you take us in small doses."

"True." And then he kissed her, and she sighed into him, wrapping her arms around his neck as he put his hands on her ass and pulled her closer.

Roxie could do this for hours, days. Just be with Carter and enjoy the scenery and just being alone. Here, they didn't have any worries, they didn't have to deal with work or family. It was just the two of them.

It was exactly what they needed.

Because it was time to talk.

It was time to just be.

And it was past time to leave it all in the open so they could move on.

Because Roxie really wanted to move on. She wanted that next part of her future.

"Let's get inside and see what else this cabin has to offer. Because I don't really think we can call it a cabin if it has two stories. And it looks to be on a hill, so there's like a basement. It's a little ridiculous."

"Yes, a cabin in the woods this is not. It's more like a mansion made out of wood in the woods. I'm a little worried."

Carter moved their bags in even though she could have helped. He liked doing things for her, and she was going to let him. Because she hadn't let him do much for her in the past, constantly pushing him away so she could prove that she was independent and do things for herself. She knew that was cutting off her nose to spite her face.

The inside of the cabin was even more beautiful than the outside. It was a stunning work of art, all gleaming wood and new appliances that somehow melded with the outdoor-esque feel of the whole place. There were huge, leather couches built for a large family or more. There were a few seating areas, as well as a loft section on one side of the house, an open-concept area with huge, vaulted ceilings in another. On the back end of the dwelling was where the rest of the rooms were located, and Roxie knew from what Liam had told her that there was even a gaming area with a couple of bedrooms in the basement. She probably wouldn't want to stay in those because there were absolutely no windows and it would be dark and kind of creepy.

It would already be creepy in the dark in a cabin in the woods, she really didn't want to be stuck in a basement at the same time.

The two of them quickly put their bags into the master bedroom, though they didn't spend any time inside, laughing and talking to each other instead of looking around. They both knew that there would be time for that later. Instead, they explored the house, looking around all the different rooms and at everything Liam owned. Roxie knew that he likely shared this with his siblings, but he was the sole owner of the place. It had to be nice having something like this. Maybe one day when her family was ready to stop expanding their businesses, they could do something like this, too. She knew her parents would probably enjoy it.

"Do you want to go for a walk before the snow really hits?" Carter asked. "I know we're up in the mountains, and it's already starting to snow a bit, so we'll probably be snowed in for the night. The app says only a couple of inches, but you know these mountains. Better safe than sorry. We'll snuggle by the fire when we get home."

Roxie kissed his jaw, though her heart clutched at the word *fire*. "I think I can do that."

He kissed her nose. "Hey, baby, I'm okay. You don't need to flinch when I say the word fire. I promise. I'm fine."

He was. She knew that. But she really didn't like to think about fire when it came to Carter. She still had nightmares of when he was burned and that he hadn't healed as much as he had. She had night terrors about a lot of things, but these days, at least, when she turned over, Carter was there. He didn't stay over every night, but once they were done with this trip, she hoped that he would move back in. Though that was something she needed to talk with him about after they'd finished everything else. Because this trip was about reconnecting, about becoming *them* again. And they were well on their way to making that happen.

They bundled up in their coats and scarves and hats and even put on hiking boots, although she had to put on new ones that weren't completely broken in yet. The ones she loved had finally gotten a hole in the bottom, and there was no fixing that. So, she put on a couple of Band-Aids and hoped for the best.

Roxie inhaled the crisp scent of the outdoors, knowing it was one of her favorite things. For someone who worked indoors and worked with numbers every single day, she sure loved being outside and in nature. It was the same way for Carter, she knew, although he was so easygoing, sometimes she thought he might be great in a big city or even in a place like this. He just fit in anywhere—even though she knew that he didn't always feel that way.

The snow fell a little bit harder as they made their way back, and Roxie had a feeling they were going to have to bundle up a little tighter tonight just in case the power went out.

"We should hurry," Carter said over the now near-blowing snow. "I checked the weather app before we left, but this is apparently coming on a little faster than expected. In fact, I think it might be a few more inches than just the two to three the weatherman said it was going to be up here."

"I know Liam wanted us to be all romantic, but I don't think being snowed in is something I really want to do."

"I'm totally with you there," Carter said with a laugh. "The whole snowed-in thing only works in books. Not so much in real life."

So, the two of them moved a little faster, she holding onto him when they went down a steeper incline that was a little bit slippery. He was just taller, and his longer legs took up the space easier than hers could. But because she was looking at those legs of his, and his very nice ass, she didn't see the root that came out of nowhere.

So, when her foot and her new shoe got caught in it, she winced at the pain before it quickly went away and she slammed into the ground. Carter had reached out to try and help her, but there was already snow and ice beneath them, making it hard for him to get to her.

Her pulse raced, and she blinked, rolling over so she could sit up easier.

"Ow," she said, rubbing her butt. "I'm fine. Just twisted my ankle."

"Shit, Roxie. You scared the hell out of me. Are you really okay?"

"I kind of scared myself, too. But I can see the lights for the house, so we're fine. Just help me up?"

"Let me check your ankle first."

"Just don't take off my shoe, you know...just in case."

"I've watched the movies and read those books. I think I know what I'm doing. Maybe."

He felt around her ankle, and she didn't even wince. She knew it wasn't a break. Probably not even a sprain. Once they'd confirmed that, he kissed her hard and then helped her up to her feet.

"The house is right there, so you're going to have to deal with this," Carter said before he lifted her up and pulled her to his chest.

She let out a squeak and wrapped her arms around his neck. "What do you think you're doing? We could trip again. I don't want you to hurt yourself."

"I'm going to carry my wife back to the house like I'm a caveman. And you're going to let me do it. The path is pretty good the rest of the way. You just happened to find the last root on the way to the house."

"Of course, I did. Because I'm me."

"I'm surprised I haven't tripped yet." And then he looked down at his feet, pausing to make sure that he didn't.

Despite her fall, they were laughing when they walked into the house, and her ankle didn't hurt at all. Yes, it was snowing, and they were going to have to put a few more logs on the fire, but it would be nice to be in a cabin in the woods during the final snowfall of the season.

At least she hoped it was the final one. Because she was ready for spring. She was ready for new beginnings. And she was ready for her husband.

He held her close as they made their way to the master bedroom and, despite it all, she smiled when she noticed the rose petals on the bed. When he set her down on top of them, he leaned forward and rested his head on hers.

"You know, if he wasn't your cousin..." he growled, though there was a smile in his tone.

"Okay, now you're starting to cross a weird line."

Carter just shook his head and kissed her softly. "First, I'm glad that you're okay right now. That you didn't hurt yourself when you fell. And, second? I'm glad that he took care of you. I'm just sorry that it had to happen at all."

Her heart ached, but it didn't feel as hollow as it had. With each conversation, with each move toward the future, Roxie was healing. But first, she had to make something clear. "I don't know if I can be really sorry."

Carter tilted his head, staring at her. "What do you mean?"

She let out a breath. "I think we needed time apart to realize what we were doing to each other. I wish we could go back and not make that happen, but then we would have to go back and make the reasons for everything not happen, and we can't do that. So, we are looking forward, and I appreciate that we're talking about everything that passed. I know I'm not making a lot of sense."

Carter just sat down next to her and held her close, tucking her into his side as he kissed the top of her head. She shivered, her heart racing at just the thought of losing him.

"You're making perfect sense. And I get what you're saying, and I actually agree with it. I hated walking out. I hated leaving you. I hated seeing those damn papers."

Papers. The papers that had started them down this new path and yet had almost ruined everything. Her hands shook, and her palms turned clammy just thinking about them. She swallowed hard.

"I hate those papers. I never signed them. So, we're still married." It felt so trivial to say that. As if they hadn't gone through the gauntlet. As if she hadn't thought of her life without him.

As if he hadn't tried to do the same.

"That's good." He let out a sigh. "I'm sorry I signed them at all. I thought it was what we needed to do, what *I* needed to do. I was wrong."

"We were wrong about a lot of things."

An understatement.

"How about we pour some wine and talk about

what we've been trying not to talk about all this time." Carter cupped her face after he'd said the words, and she leaned into him, knowing it was beyond time.

"I think we need to."

And so he took her hand and led her from the master bedroom into the kitchen. Liam had also left her favorite wine out on the counter, a pinot noir that she knew was pretty hard to get in this state.

"Apparently, he really wants us to stay together. Plying us with wine and rose petals. I'm pretty sure I spotted some chocolates in the fridge, too."

"He's a good man. I promise I don't want to hit him." Carter ran his hands down her sides, and she wondered why she was so nervous. This wasn't the first time they'd brought up uncomfortable subjects, but it was the first time they were actually doing it on purpose. At least, about this particular subject.

"That's good, because he is family."

They went into the living room, holding their glasses of wine before setting them down. She'd taken a single sip of hers, but he hadn't touched his. Maybe they needed their wits about them to talk, but she needed that single sip to push her in the right direction.

Maybe if she talked quickly, it wouldn't hurt so badly. "I remember the day I found out I was pregnant. I remember it so clearly."

She was wrong.

It hurt.

It hurt so damn much.

The only thing that hurt more was when she'd thought Carter had died...and when she'd thought she lost him forever.

Carter ran his hands over his face, his eyes dark and focused on the past, his devastation clear. "Me, too. I was so damn nervous and excited and scared. We hadn't even talked about kids. At least not in reality. It had always been in the abstract, as something we might want to do if we got married."

"And then I was pregnant, and we didn't tell my parents. We didn't tell my family. We didn't tell anyone. It was just you and me, and this little baby that was going to come and change everything." She put her hands over her stomach, remembering what it was like to feel something growing inside of her. Though she hadn't made it to the months where she could fully feel her baby kick. Maybe a flutter, but she had never truly known the joy.

She had lost the baby before it had become truly real, but in the end, it had been real enough that it had ruined part of her. Shattered the parts that made her Roxie, devastated the part that had made her want to be with her husband. Or rather destroyed the part that had made her think that she *could be* with her husband.

"I will never forget the day that I walked into the house and saw you bleeding on the floor." Carter's voice was rough as he spoke, and it pulled her out of her thoughts.

"I don't remember much about you picking me up."

"I honestly thought you were dead. You were covered in blood, and your hands were out as if you were trying to get to your phone, but it had fallen when you hit the floor. And I had just come home early from work because I had a shitty day and just wanted to see you. And then you were on the floor, and I thought I'd lost you."

"You almost did."

When she had the miscarriage, her body hadn't been able to let her know that she was actually losing her baby until it was too late. She would have died if Carter hadn't called the ambulance right then. If he hadn't been there when she needed him.

And she'd pushed him away because she'd been scared.

And he'd stayed away because he hadn't known how to help.

"Everything changed." Her voice was hollow again, but she knew she could feel. That's all she could do.

"When I heard that you lost the baby, I wasn't relieved, but it was more that you were there for me, *with* me. I wasn't going to lose you, too."

"I grieved. I woke up, and I knew that our baby was gone. And it scared me. It scared me because I was afraid that we had gotten married because of that baby. And then you were going to leave me. And then I didn't know if we wanted to have a baby right away or if we should even start trying. And so, we didn't talk about it. I just said that I wanted to get an IUD, and you said okay. And we didn't talk. That was so stupid of me. It was so stupid of us."

"So fucking stupid," Carter agreed. "I don't even..." He let out a breath. "I don't even know what to say anymore. I feel like all I'm doing is saying the wrong things, at least that's how it used to be. Because you just turned in on yourself when we lost the baby. You didn't tell your family, and I knew it wasn't my place to tell them. And I didn't fight you to do anything about it. I just thought you were moving on and figured I should, too."

"I just...I was just trying to figure out exactly who I was. Because I know we've said that we got married because of who we are together and the fact that we love each other. And, yes, maybe we did rush into the wedding a little early, but you were going to propose. I know that now. But I didn't know that before. I didn't know that you asked me to marry you when you did because of me and not because of the pregnancy. And so, I had this idea in my head that I needed to have another baby to make sure that everything was just fine, and we could make it work. And then I knew I wasn't ready, and I didn't know when or if I would be, so I went on birth control. And you were okay with it. I just didn't understand."

Carter kissed her, kissed away her tears though they didn't come. "And you didn't ask. But then again, I didn't either. I didn't want to hurt you by making you think of what we'd lost. Because I missed that baby so much. We didn't even name it. The doctors said it was so early that we just...we didn't do what we needed to."

Tears finally ran down her face at his words.

"I always thought of her as Angel in my head."

He kissed her then, and she let the tears fall. "I know." She broke. "You whispered it in your sleep. I tried to hold you, and you pushed me away. And then I didn't know how to talk to you anymore. I didn't know how I felt anymore. We lost our Angel...and I didn't know what to do."

She wiped away his tears this time and kissed his cheeks. She loved this man, loved the way he felt things so deeply.

They had been so scared before, so broken, that they hadn't known how to deal with their grief.

"We need to talk about Angel more. The baby we lost. It wasn't her that brought us together. That's what I thought for so long, and because of that, I almost lost you. But I love you so much. So, can we just be us? Can we talk about Angel more? And can we just be us?"

He picked her up and put her on his lap and held her close. "I love you, Roxie Montgomery-Marshall. I love you to the very depths of my soul. And we should have talked about Angel long before this. We should have talked about the fact that we lost something so precious, and not only our baby. We lost us. I don't want to do that again. So, I want to use this weekend, and I want to just love you. Forever. Can you make that happen? Can we?"

"I know forevers aren't something that's promised. But I want to try. I want to be with you for as forever as forever can be. And, yes, let's talk about Angel."

So, for the rest of the night, they talked about the angel that they never got to hold, the angel Roxie had almost died for. They talked about the blood on the floor, the blood on his hands.

And she promised him that they would talk to her family soon about it. Because they were talking to each other. They were together.

Sure, it was scary, but they were making it work, and they could maybe have another baby in the future. But that would come with time.

But first, first Roxie just needed her husband. She needed that forever.

And with Carter, she knew she could find it.

Finally.

CHAPTER EIGHTEEN

Carter slid his clothes into the dresser drawer, closing it with a soft snap. As soon as he did, his shoulders immediately relaxed, and he let out a breath.

He'd moved back in.

Finally.

He knew it wasn't over, they still had to work on their marriage, but now they would be doing it under the same roof.

The two of them were in the middle of their new beginning. Or maybe they were just starting. Either way, there was more to do than just pretending that everything would be okay if they continued to talk. They would continue to talk. Carter was more in love with Roxie now than he had ever been before. And he was going to make sure that they kept up with their newly found counseling sessions. Yes, they would be going to marriage counseling. But it was more than that. They were going to start grief counseling, too.

It was something they should've done long before this. It was something they should've done before they walked away from each other emotionally, before they did so physically, too.

Carter had never been one to talk about his feelings. He had hidden himself from the dangers of what it meant to feel long before he even met Roxie. She had been the one to open him up after he lost his parents. Roxie had done so much for him.

Now, he was going to do something good for both of them and make sure he continued to be open with his wife.

And that meant counseling. That meant talking. And that meant facing his fears.

Because, in the end, he was just so afraid that he was going to lose his wife again. He knew that if he weren't careful, he would make more mistakes. So, going to an outside source, and even talking to her family, *his* family, would help.

"Are you okay in there?" Roxie asked, her voice not as hesitant as it had been. Because they were together, and this was their happily ever after.

Finally.

"Yeah, one sec."

He quickly put the last of his things away and then went to the living room. Roxie sat there on the couch, a cheese plate in front of her, and a smile on her face.

"You know, I really don't think it's just Thea who likes cheese to that shocking degree anymore. I'm pretty sure you have joined the ranks."

"She's the one who sent the cheese over. I can't help that I had to cut it up and have it with grapes and some crackers and a little thing of nuts. A charcuterie plate needs to be set if there's cheese in the house."

"*One of us. One of us. One of us.*"

She tossed a pillow at him, and he caught it, grinning. And then he leaned over and kissed her lips. "I love you, Roxie."

"I love you more, Carter."

"No, I don't think that's possible. But we can be equal. How's that?"

She snuggled up to him and kissed his jaw. He loved when she did that. And he knew that she liked it when he had a beard, so he had started doing extra beard care on his newly grown facial hair. That meant more time working on his face in the morning, and the guys sometimes razzed him about it at the shop when they could smell the sandalwood or whatever other scents he knew Roxie might like. He didn't care. Because Roxie liked it, and that was all that mattered. And if he were honest with himself, he liked it, too.

"Are you ready?" he asked, his voice soft.

"I've been ready." Her eyes filled with tears, but she blinked them away, so he kissed each cheekbone and then the tip of her nose. And then they both leaned forward to the stack of papers next to the cheese plate. One by one, they tore up each sheet. Yes, the fact that she had filed would forever be on some computer somewhere for people to find, but that didn't matter. This was just a symbol of what him moving back in meant. They were no longer getting a divorce. The idea that he had signed the papers at all because he had thought he wasn't good enough, that it was what they needed, just brought them closer in the end.

Maybe they had gone about it the wrong way, but he didn't care.

They had gone about it their way and were now going to be just fine.

Thank God.

As soon as the final paper was torn, he started kissing her again. Then she was on her back, and he was between her legs, rocking into her as he kissed her. Both of their breaths came in pants, and he was just about to lift up her sweater—wine, cheese, and paper shreds long forgotten—when Roxie's phone buzzed on the table. They both froze, looking at each other, and then started laughing. They had tried to have sex at least four times that day, and a different family member had called every single time.

Everyone was just so happy that they were getting back together, that they were finally back together, that the phone hadn't stopped ringing.

"I'm never going to be able to get inside you again, am I?"

She just smiled and patted his chest, so he sat up and brought her with him. He kissed her again as she reached for the phone, but when she answered, she was straddling him, and his hard cock was pressed against her heat. It didn't matter that they were both wearing pants. It had to count for something.

"Hey, Shea, how are you today?"

Carter just laughed, trying to keep it silent because her sister-in-law calling was just one of many. Landon had actually been the first person to call that morning, surprising both of them. But his former roommate had mentioned that he had left a sock over, and Carter would have to be back soon to get it.

He had a feeling Landon missed him, even if neither of them would say it. He would never be able to truly give back and say thanks when it came to what Landon had done for him. He had not only forced Carter to look at what he was leaving but had given him shelter from the rain. Metaphorically and physically. Carter just hoped to be able to repay the favor one day, and with the way things were going with Kaylee and Landon, that might happen soon.

"Let me put you on speaker," Roxie said quickly, her eyes wide. There was something off about that. Carter could sense the happiness in her tone, but it was like she was pulling away again for some reason. He didn't understand it. But as soon as Shea said the words, he understood.

"Shep and I are having another baby!"

Another baby.

It didn't hurt, not like he thought it would, because he was happy for them. But, still.

"Congratulations," he said, his gaze on Roxie's. Because she was saying all the right words, doing all the right things, but something was...off. And he didn't know what.

"I'm just so happy for you," Roxie said. "So, when's the big day?"

Shea began to talk, talking about going into second trimesters, and how proud the daddy was. Shep was in the background, grumbling about having to deal with two children, even though he sounded beyond happy.

Shep just liked to complain with a growl because he knew that Shea would just lap it up, grinning and laughing with her husband.

Carter said all the right things along with Roxie, knowing that he was going to love this baby just like he loved Livvy and Daisy and any other children that came into their lives that he would be an uncle to.

But he still felt that little clutch, the idea that their baby hadn't made it. The idea that he and Roxie didn't have *their* baby. Their Angel.

And maybe that was what was wrong with Roxie. But there was something different there, something more than just the pain he knew she must be feeling.

And so when they hung up, he leaned forward, but she scrambled off his lap, her hands shaking. "What's wrong?"

She didn't answer. So, Carter guessed. "Shep and Shea said that they had been trying for another baby for the past year, and it's finally happening. Are you thinking about Angel? I am, too, but what else is wrong, Roxie?"

"I don't know if I can do this. I didn't know it would hurt this much. I...I can't breathe." And then she walked out of the room, leaving him alone and wondering what the fuck had just happened.

Wait. This wasn't going to end like this. She wasn't

just going to walk out of the room. They were going to talk. They had worked way too hard for this, and he was done not talking about the big things. He didn't care if it hurt. So, he followed her into the bedroom where she paced, wrapping her arms around her middle.

"Talk to me. We made a promise to each other, Roxie. Fucking talk to me."

"I know. And I didn't mean to actually walk away from you, I just needed space to breathe. Not space from you."

He cupped her face, stalling her pacing. "Tell me what you're thinking."

"I don't know if I even want another baby. And I don't know why those thoughts are coming to me when I'm thinking about Shep and Shea, because that has nothing to do with me. I'm like the most selfish sister in the world."

Carter took a breath, letting her words soak into him, and then he nodded. "Okay. We're getting some-where. You are not selfish for thinking about yourself."

"That is the definition of being selfish."

"No, it isn't. You're not only thinking about you. Because I know you were genuine when you said that you were happy for them. I know that because I see the way you act around Livvy. The way you act around

Daisy. Daisy isn't even technically our niece yet, and you still act like the best aunt in the world."

"I think that my sisters and Shea might disagree with that."

"No, you're all collectively the best aunts in the world. You're damn good at what you do, and you love those little girls. And you're going to love this new baby. And you're going to love any other babies that come into the Montgomerys. You're allowed to think about more than just that at once. You are a beautiful, brilliant, and dynamic woman. You can think about many things and care about many things at once. That's what makes you human. That's what makes us human. But let's talk about that thing you said first. You don't know if you ever want a baby?"

She shook her head, and he knew that she was going to be sick soon if she didn't let it out. He knew his wife. He could read her again. Because she wasn't closing herself off. And that counted for more than anything.

"Talk to me."

She breathed against him before she spoke. "When I got pregnant the first time, I was excited but scared. Because having a kid was always something that was just on the periphery." She ran her hands over her face.

"And then when we lost her, I went to a support group. You know that. We talked about it."

He nodded. At the cabin, they had talked about the fact that Roxie had gone right after losing the baby. But she hadn't said what had happened there, only that she had tried, and it hadn't worked out.

"What happened?"

"There were so many women there who desperately wanted to be mothers. And it was like they were feeding into each other, trying to explain to each other that all they wanted in this world was to be a mother. That their entire identity of being a woman was to become a mother. And it hurt. Because I knew that wasn't the case for them. And I know it's not the case for me. My identity is more than just that, and it scares me and makes me feel like a horrible person. Because I know that we are layered, made up of so many different things, and I was truly afraid that I was drowning in something that I didn't understand."

Carter nodded, letting her speak. He didn't know what to say because he'd never felt like that, hadn't had the world put on his shoulders that way. But he'd missed it in Roxie, and that was something he would have to help with. If she let him.

"There was this woman who looked directly at me as she was speaking, though I know she was talking to the whole group. She said that by not having our babies, the ones we lost, we were not fulfilling our purpose in life. I knew that was bullshit. I wanted that baby, sure. I wanted Angel so badly once I knew it was a possibility. But now... now, I know that we need to figure out who we are. And we're on that path, and we're doing it, and I love you so much. But I'm this confused, tangled mess of nerves, and this woman's words just keep coming back to me."

Carter let out a breath and then kissed her before putting his hands on her shoulders, looking her directly in the eyes. Anger coursed through him, but he let it go. This wasn't about him. It never had been. "What that woman said was bullshit. You're right. And because of those words, they're making you all confused."

"I know. That's what I just said."

"I'm not good with words, Roxie. You know this. But I know that your worth is not tied up with just one thing. Your worth is connected to everything, and that makes me love you so much. And when we are ready to have a baby, *if* we are ready to have a baby, we will make that decision together. I'm not going to pressure you, and you're not going to pressure me. And our family, the Montgomerys—because you made a point that they are my family, too—our family won't pressure us either. Because they never did when we were fighting. They were there for us when we needed them, they were there for you when you needed them. But we'll make our own path. And when the time comes, we'll be there for each other. Because, dammit, I'm not losing you again."

"I know. It's just this whole big thing in my head, and I think I just needed to get it out. I feel so stupid."

"You're not stupid."

"But I say stupid things. And my mind goes to stupid places."

"Well, let's talk about it with our counselor." He paused. "I can't believe I just said those words out loud."

"I can't believe you did either, but I'm kind of glad you did because we're growing. We're actually being adults and dealing with what's going on inside of us. I probably should've done this long before now, but, as I said, I'm stupid sometimes. And, yes, I realize I just said I'm stupid again, but I'm running out of words for how muddled my brain feels when it comes to this whole baby thing."

"Then let's do it. One day at a time, one step at a time. Maybe we'll have kids in the future, or maybe we won't. Maybe we should start with a cat. I know you like cats."

"I love cats. And dogs. Maybe a gerbil."

He snorted. "A gerbil could work. We can find something that works."

He laughed and then kissed her again. "I love you so damn much. And I'm never going to take that for granted again."

"Deal, I love you."

"Now, let me kiss away those tears, and maybe we can get back to where we left off before the phone rang." And, as if on cue, her phone rang again, and she chuckled as she leaned her forehead against his chest.

"Okay, seems like a baby won't be a problem because we're never having sex again."

"You're a dork. I love you."

And then he took her hand, and they went into the living room to answer the call from her mother who wanted to talk about the upcoming baby.

And, one day, if they were ready, they might have a child of their own. But first, they were just going to be Roxie and Carter.

Finally.

They were their own version of themselves. Because they had taken far too long to figure out who that was, and Carter was never letting go. He had found his happily ever after, even when he had been firmly running away from it.

Roxie was his.

And he was never letting go again.

EPILOGUE

Montgomery dinners were seriously one of Roxie's favorite things, especially when they included friends of the family that were practically family members themselves. They hadn't always been, but today? Today was pretty amazing.

They were all stuffed to the gills with roast, potatoes, green beans, and rolls. And, of course, cheese since Thea and Dimitri were there. Now, they had piled into her parents' living room to talk about upcoming wedding plans for Thea and Dimitri, as well as Adrienne and Mace.

Talk of a double-wedding had come up and had been properly shut down, very quickly. After all, Thea and Adrienne could not be more different in terms of taste, and everyone wanted more than one party to celebrate their growing family.

Roxie and Carter had thought about renewing their vows to each other but had decided against it. They had said their words of promise and love and forever to each other more than once, and with each time they opened up to each other, and every time they leaned on one another, it was a vow that counted for more than any ceremony would.

They *were*, however, actually going on a honeymoon this summer. They were headed to Aruba where she could enjoy the blue waters, white sand, and watching her husband walk around in nothing but shorts that rode low on his hips.

Her mouth watered just thinking about it.

"You're drooling," Carter whispered in her ear, and she closed her eyes, knowing she was blushing.

"Shush," she whispered.

"I know you're thinking something naughty. Keep it in mind for later."

"Shush," she repeated, her face hot.

"What are you two whispering about over there?" her mom asked from the floor where she sat with Captain, Daisy, Julia, and Livvy. Her mom was seriously one amazing grandma.

"Nothing," she and Carter said at the same time,

and all of the adults in the room laughed, the kids joining in on the fun. Captain howled just for the heck of it.

This was family. This was what Roxie had run from because she'd been scared that she wasn't enough. But she'd been wrong. Oh, so wrong.

Shep and Shea were in Colorado for the long haul, and she was getting to know her brother and sister-in-law in new ways every day. Roxie smiled down at Shea's tiny baby bump and didn't feel a single ounce of whatever she had felt the day she'd found out they were having another baby. Talking it out with Carter and their counselor had helped.

Roxie hadn't realized how much those words from that one woman at a single meeting had gotten to her over the last year, and she was glad that she had been able to get it out of her head. Because she knew that, one day, she and Carter might want a baby of their own. But there was no rush. They had time and, for now, they could focus on each other, something they hadn't been able to do properly because they were both so in their heads.

Roxie looked over at Adrienne and Mace as they whispered to one another, Mace's big hand in her sister's hair. The two had been best friends for ages, and when they finally fell for each other, Roxie had cheered. They were perfect for each other, and Roxie couldn't wait to see what they did with their family as time moved on.

And that brought her to Thea and Dimitri. The two were so new in their relationship, but like Mace and Adrienne, they had been friends first. Now, they were getting married and blending their lives. And, in the best news yet of the day, Thea was officially breaking ground on her expansion at the bakery. The loan had come through, and soon, the next phase of her life would start.

Roxie's family had some serious talent, and she knew they were blessed. Yes, they'd hurt some over the years, had each gone through their own issues, but in the end, Roxie figured they'd all come out stronger.

She also knew that her family wasn't the only ones who had gone through things like that. She couldn't help but think of Liam and the issues he was dealing with, but she pushed that from her mind, knowing there was nothing she could do except be there for her cousin.

If he let her.

Roxie reached out and squeezed her husband's hand, and he kissed her temple as he kept his conversation with Landon going. Their friend had brought Kaylee with him, the couple no longer hiding their relationship. Not that they'd actually hidden it from anyone but each other before, but that was their story to tell. One she knew Kaylee would tell her. One day.

Abby and Ryan sat next to the other couple, laughing at something Roxie's father had said. Every once in a while, Julia would come up to Ryan and hand him something before going back to play with the other kids.

The two were growing closer, their relationship blooming before the family's eyes, and Roxie couldn't be happier.

Roxie leaned into her husband, looking down at her wedding rings that she'd slid back on after he kissed her in their home, knowing she was blessed. *They* were blessed. They'd gone through hell to get here, but they'd made it out.

The paperwork had been destroyed, thankfully, and she and Carter were living their forever. Though there *was* one set of paperwork they would be filing soon. Her name would no longer be hyphenated. Instead, she would just be a Marshall.

A Montgomery by birth and by blood.

But a Marshall by choice and love.

And that was exactly what she needed. Because in her heart, Roxie knew that she and Carter would always be Montgomerys.

Because in the end, you never escaped being a Montgomery.

Not even when you thought you should try.

****

Up Next:

Liam Montgomery finds his match in WRAPPED IN INK.

&

Landon & Kaylee have a special bonus romance in INK BY NUMBERS!

A NOTE FROM CARRIE ANN

Thank you so much for reading **JAGGED INK.** I do hope if you liked this story, that you would please leave a review! Reviews help authors *and* readers.

I'm so honored that you read this book and love the Montgomerys as much as I do. This book wasn't easy. It was far different than anything else I've ever written. Roxie and Carter had issues. I know this, but their romance was REAL to me and it played out how marriages sometimes turn out. Finding love when you think you don't deserve it isn't easy and I'm so happy this book came out the way it did.

And in case you missed it, you can find their brother Shep's romance in INK INSPIRED.

Mace and Adrienne were in FALLEN INK, Dimitri

and Thea in RESTLESS INK, and Abby and Ryan in ASHES TO INK.

Up next is INK BY NUMBERS, a fun and steamy novella with Landon and Kaylee.

And then I move up to Boulder to visit with Liam Montgomery and his siblings in the Montgomery Ink: Boulder series. Liam is up first in WRAPPED IN INK. And just wait, there are some SHOCKING things coming up that Liam isn't ready for.

Montgomery Ink: Colorado Springs

Book 1: Fallen Ink

Book 2: Restless Ink

Book 2.5: Ashes to Ink

Book 3: Jagged Ink

Book 3.5: Ink by Numbers

If you want to make sure you know what's coming next from me, you can sign up for my newsletter at www. CarrieAnnRyan.com; follow me on twitter at @CarrieAnnRyan, or like my Facebook page. I also have a Facebook Fan Club where we have trivia, chats, and other goodies. You guys are the reason I get to do what I do and I thank you.

Make sure you're signed up for my MAILING LIST so

you can know when the next releases are available as well as find giveaways and FREE READS.

Happy Reading!

ALSO FROM CARRIE ANN RYAN

The Montgomery Ink Legacy Series:

Book 1: Bittersweet Promises (Leif & Brooke)

Book 2: At First Meet (Nick & Lake)

Book 2.5: Happily Ever Never (May & Leo)

Book 3: Longtime Crush (Sebastian & Raven)

Book 4: Best Friend Temptation (Noah, Ford, and Greer)

Book 4.5: Happily Ever Maybe (Jennifer & Gus)

Book 5: Last First Kiss (Daisy & Hugh)

Book 6: His Second Chance (Kane & Phoebe)

Book 7: One Night with You (Kingston & Claire)

Book 8: Accidentally Forever (Crew & Aria)

Book 9: Last Chance Seduction (Lexington & Mercy)

Book 10: Kiss Me Forever (Brooklyn & Reece)

Book 11: His Guilty Pleasure (Dash & Aly)

Book 12: Maybe it's You (Riley & Gage)

The Cage Family

Book 1: The Forever Rule (Aston & Blakely)

Book 2: An Unexpected Everything (Isabella & Weston)

Book 3: If You Were Mine (Dorian & Harper)

Book 4: One Quick Obsession (Hudson & Scarlett)

Book 5: Pretend it's Forever (Sophia & Carson)

Book 6: Wish it Were You (Flynn & Luna)

Ashford Creek

Book 1: Legacy (Callum & Felicity)

Book 2: Crossroads (Bodhi & Kiera)

Book 3: Westward (Atlas & Elizabeth)

Book 4: Patience (Teagan & Rush)

Clover Lake

Book 1: Always a Fake Bridesmaid (Livvy & Ewan)

Book 2: Accidental Runaway Groom (Jamie & Sharp)

Book 3: His Practically Fake Proposal (Galen & Addy)

The Wilder Brothers Series:

Book 1: One Way Back to Me (Eli & Alexis)

Book 2: Always the One for Me (Evan & Kendall)

Book 3: The Path to You (Everett & Bethany)

Book 4: Coming Home for Us (Elijah & Maddie)

Book 5: Stay Here With Me (East & Lark)

Book 6: Finding the Road to Us (Elliot, Trace, and Sidney)

Book 7: Moments for You (Ridge & Aurora)

Book 7.5: A Wilder Wedding (Amos & Naomi)

Book 8: Forever For Us (Wyatt & Ava)

Book 9: Pieces of Me (Gabriel & Briar)

Book 10: Endlessly Yours (Brooks & Rory)

The Falling for the Cassidy Brothers Series:

(Formerly the First Time Series)

Book 1: Good Time Boyfriend (Heath & Devney)

Book 2: Last Minute Fiancé (Luca & Addison)

Book 3: Second Chance Husband (August & Paisley)

Montgomery Ink Denver:

Book 0.5: Ink Inspired (Shep & Shea)

Book 0.6: Ink Reunited (Sassy, Rare, and Ian)

Book 1: Delicate Ink (Austin & Sierra)

Book 1.5: Forever Ink (Callie & Morgan)

Book 2: Tempting Boundaries (Decker and Miranda)

Book 3: Harder than Words (Meghan & Luc)

Book 3.5: <u>Finally Found You </u>(Mason & Presley)

Book 4: <u>Written in Ink </u>(Griffin & Autumn)

Book 4.5: <u>Hidden Ink </u>(Hailey & Sloane)

Book 5: <u>Ink Enduring </u>(Maya, Jake, and Border)

Book 6: <u>Ink Exposed </u>(Alex & Tabby)

Book 6.5: <u>Adoring Ink </u>(Holly & Brody)

Book 6.6: <u>Love, Honor, & Ink </u>(Arianna & Harper)

Book 7: <u>Inked Expressions </u>(Storm & Everly)

Book 7.3: <u>Dropout </u>(Grayson & Kate)

Book 7.5: <u>Executive Ink </u>(Jax & Ashlynn)

Book 8: <u>Inked Memories </u>(Wes & Jillian)

Book 8.5: <u>Inked Nights </u>(Derek & Olivia)

Book 8.7: <u>Second Chance Ink </u>(Brandon & Lauren)

Book 8.5: Montgomery Midnight Kisses (Alex & Tabby Bonus(

Bonus: Inked Kingdom (Stone & Sarina)

Montgomery Ink: Colorado Springs

Book 1: Fallen Ink (Adrienne & Mace)

Book 2: Restless Ink (Thea & Dimitri)

Book 2.5: Ashes to Ink (Abby & Ryan)

Book 3: Jagged Ink (Roxie & Carter)

Book 3.5: Ink by Numbers (Landon & Kaylee)

The Montgomery Ink: Boulder Series:

Book 1: Wrapped in Ink (Liam & Arden)

Book 2: Sated in Ink (Ethan, Lincoln, and Holland)

Book 3: Embraced in Ink (Bristol & Marcus)

Book 3: Moments in Ink (Zia & Meredith)

Book 4: Seduced in Ink (Aaron & Madison)

Book 4.5: Captured in Ink (Julia, Ronin, & Kincaid)

Book 4.7: Inked Fantasy (Secret ??)

Book 4.8: A Very Montgomery Christmas (The Entire Boulder Family)

The Montgomery Ink: Fort Collins Series:

Book 1: Inked Persuasion (Jacob & Annabelle)

Book 2: Inked Obsession (Beckett & Eliza)

Book 3: Inked Devotion (Benjamin & Brenna)

Book 3.5: Nothing But Ink (Clay & Riggs)

Book 4: Inked Craving (Lee & Paige)

Book 5: Inked Temptation (Archer & Killian)

The Promise Me Series:

Book 1: Forever Only Once (Cross & Hazel)

Book 2: From That Moment (Prior & Paris)

Book 3: Far From Destined (Macon & Dakota)

Book 4: From Our First (Nate & Myra)

The Whiskey and Lies Series:

Book 1: Whiskey Secrets (Dare & Kenzie)

Book 2: Whiskey Reveals (Fox & Melody)

Book 3: <u>Whiskey Undone</u> (Loch & Ainsley)

The Gallagher Brothers Series:

Book 1: <u>Love Restored</u> (Graham & Blake)

Book 2: <u>Passion Restored</u> (Owen & Liz)

Book 3: <u>Hope Restored</u> (Murphy & Tessa)

The Carr Family Series:

(Formerly the Less Than Series)

Book 1: Breathless With Her (Devin & Erin)

Book 2: Reckless With You (Tucker & Amelia)

Book 3: Shameless With Him (Caleb & Zoey)

The Fractured Connections Series:

Book 1: Breaking Without You (Cameron & Violet)

Book 2: Shouldn't Have You (Brendon & Harmony)

Book 3: Falling With You (Aiden & Sienna)

Book 4: Taken With You (Beckham & Meadow)

The Campus Roommates Series:

(Formerly the On My Own Series)

Book 0.5: My First Glance

Book 1: My One Night (Dillon & Elise)

Book 2: My Rebound (Pacey & Mackenzie)

Book 3: My Next Play (Miles & Nessa)

Book 4: My Bad Decisions (Tanner & Natalie)

The Ravenwood Coven Series:

Book 1: Dawn Unearthed

Book 2: Dusk Unveiled

Book 3: Evernight Unleashed

The Aspen Pack Series:

Book 1: Etched in Honor

Book 2: Hunted in Darkness

Book 3: Mated in Chaos

Book 4: Harbored in Silence

Book 5: Marked in Flames

The Talon Pack:

Book 1: Tattered Loyalties

Book 2: An Alpha's Choice

Book 3: Mated in Mist

Book 4: Wolf Betrayed

Book 5: Fractured Silence

Book 6: Destiny Disgraced

Book 7: Eternal Mourning

Book 8: Strength Enduring

Book 9: Forever Broken

Book 10: Mated in Darkness

Book 11: Fated in Winter

Redwood Pack Series:

Book 0.5: <u>An Alpha's Path</u>

Book 1: <u>A Taste for a Mate</u>

Book 2: <u>Trinity Bound</u>

Book 2.5: <u>A Night Away</u>

Book 3: <u>Enforcer's Redemption</u>

Book 3.5: <u>Blurred Expectations</u>

Book 3.7: <u>Forgiveness</u>

Book 4: <u>Shattered Emotions</u>

Book 5: <u>Hidden Destiny</u>

Book 5.5: <u>A Beta's Haven</u>

Book 6: <u>Fighting Fate</u>

Book 6.5: <u>Loving the Omega</u>

Book 6.7: <u>The Hunted Heart</u>

Book 7: <u>Wicked Wolf</u>

The Elements of Five Series:

Book 1: From Breath and Ruin

Book 2: From Flame and Ash

Book 3: From Spirit and Binding

Book 4: From Shadow and Silence

Dante's Circle Series:

Book 1: <u>Dust of My Wings</u>

Book 2: <u>Her Warriors' Three Wishes</u>

Book 3: <u>An Unlucky Moon</u>

Book 3.5: <u>His Choice</u>

Book 4: <u>Tangled Innocence</u>

Book 5: <u>Fierce Enchantment</u>

Book 6: <u>An Immortal's Song</u>

Book 7: <u>Prowled Darkness</u>

Book 8: Dante's Circle Reborn

Holiday, Montana Series:

Book 1: <u>Charmed Spirits</u>

Book 2: <u>Santa's Executive</u>

Book 3: <u>Finding Abigail</u>

Book 4: <u>Her Lucky Love</u>

Book 5: Dreams of Ivory

The Branded Pack Series:

(Written with Alexandra Ivy)

Book 1: <u>Stolen and Forgiven</u>

Book 2: <u>Abandoned and Unseen</u>

Book 3: <u>Buried and Shadowed</u>

ABOUT THE AUTHOR

Carrie Ann Ryan is the New York Times and USA Today bestselling author of contemporary, paranormal, and young adult romance. Her works include the Montgomery Ink, Redwood Pack, Fractured Connections, and Elements of Five series, which have sold over 3.0 million books worldwide. She started writing while in graduate school for her advanced degree in chemistry and hasn't stopped since. Carrie Ann has written over seventy-five novels and novellas with more in the works. When she's not losing herself in her emotional and action-packed worlds, she's reading as much as she can while wrangling her clowder of cats who have more followers than she does.

www.CarrieAnnRyan.com